THE YS TALES

WHISPERS OF WISDOM

YS YADAV

Made with ♥ on the Notion Press Platform
www.notionpress.com

All the parents and grandparents who, with unwavering love, continue the timeless tradition of storytelling, their voices weaving magic and wisdom into the hearts of their children and grandchildren.

Those who have inspired generations with their stories of courage, resilience, and the unwavering pursuit of their dreams, their lives a testament to the boundless potential of the human spirit.

The great souls whose words, like guiding stars, continue to illuminate our paths, offering solace, wisdom, and unwavering support when we find ourselves at the crossroads of life.

Contents

Contents

Epigraph

"The world whispers its wisdom to those who listen with an
open heart."

Preface

Dear Reader, Welcome to "The YS Tales: Whispers of Wisdom," a collection of stories that I hope will spark your imagination, touch your heart, and leave you with a deeper understanding of the human experience.

These stories were born from a desire to share the wisdom I've gleaned over the years, the lessons I've learned from my own experiences, and the insights I've gained from observing the world around me. Each tale is a journey, an exploration of the challenges and triumphs, the joys and sorrows, the hopes and fears that shape our lives.

Within these pages, you'll encounter a diverse cast of characters - farmers and teachers, artists and entrepreneurs, mothers and fathers, children and grandparents. You'll journey with them through bustling cities and quiet villages, across ancient landscapes and modern metropolises, as they navigate the complexities of life, love, loss, and the pursuit of happiness.

These stories are not just about entertainment; they are about reflection, about finding meaning in the midst of chaos, about discovering the strength and resilience that lie within us all. They are about the whispers of wisdom that guide us, the unspoken truths that connect us, and the enduring power of the human spirit to overcome adversity and create a better world.

As you turn the pages of this book, I invite you to listen with an open heart, to allow the stories to resonate with your own experiences, and to discover the whispers of wisdom that lie hidden within each tale.

Thank you for joining me on this journey. I hope you find these stories as enriching and inspiring as I have found them to be.

Introduction

Welcome, dear reader, to "The YS Tales: Whispers of Wisdom," a collection of stories that invites you to explore the depths of human experience, to discover the hidden truths that lie within us all, and to embrace the transformative power of wisdom.

Within these pages, you will embark on a journey through a tapestry of tales, each one a unique exploration of the challenges and triumphs that shape our lives. You will encounter characters from all walks of life - farmers and teachers, artists and entrepreneurs, mothers and fathers, children and grandparents - as they navigate the complexities of love, loss, ambition, and the pursuit of happiness.

You will witness the resilience of the human spirit in "The Arrow of the Past," as a young hunter learns to let go of the wounds of the past and embrace the healing power of forgiveness. You will confront the insidious nature of greed in "The Greedy Shadow," and discover the true meaning of wealth in "The Wealth of Integrity."

In "The Mirror of Incompatible Reflections," you will be reminded of the importance of self-acceptance and the unique value that each individual brings to the world. You will witness the awakening of a soul in "The Awakening," and the power of silent support in "The Silent Observer."

The bonds of friendship and family will be celebrated in "The Unbreakable Bond" and "The Banyan Bond," while the courage to defy expectations and pursue one's dreams will be illuminated in "The Jasmine's Unfolding" and "The Courage to Bloom."

You will delve into the complexities of ambition and its consequences in "The Cost of Ambition" and "The Fall of a Titan," and you will be inspired by the unwavering commitment to justice in "The Price of Integrity" and "The Halls of Silence."

The power of silence and introspection will be revealed in "The Unspoken Power" and "The Inner Pilgrimage," while the enduring nature of love and legacy will be explored in "Footprints in the Moonlight" and "The Unseen Goodbye."

Through these stories and many more, you will be invited to reflect on the deeper meaning of life, to question your own beliefs and values, and to discover the whispers of wisdom that can guide you on your own unique journey.

So, dear reader, turn the page and embark on this adventure of self-discovery and enlightenment. Allow the stories to touch your heart, to challenge your mind, and to awaken the wisdom that lies within you.

May the whispers of wisdom guide you, and may the tales you encounter within these pages inspire you to live a life filled with purpose, meaning, and the unwavering pursuit of your own truth.

I

The Arrow of the Past

"The past is an arrow already flown; wisdom lies in learning from its flight, not chasing its return."

The Whispers of the Ancients

The ancient forest breathed around Arjun, a living entity of rustling leaves and whispering winds. He moved through its depths with the easy grace of one who belonged, his bare feet barely disturbing the carpet of fallen leaves. Arjun was a son of these woods, his life intertwined with its rhythms, his spirit attuned to its secrets. He knew its paths as well as he knew the lines on his own hand, its moods as intimately as he knew the beat of his own heart. Yet, today, a shadow lingered in the sun-dappled glades, a disquiet that tugged at the edges of his calm. It was a whisper from the past, a memory that clung to him like the morning mist, refusing to dissipate.

The Echo of the Arrow

His bow, crafted from the heartwood of a fallen oak, felt heavier than usual in his hand. It was a legacy from his father, a hunter renowned throughout the region, a man whose laughter had once echoed through these very trees. But the laughter had been silenced, cut short by the cruel whisper of a stray arrow, a tragedy that had etched itself into Arjun's soul. He wasn't just hunting today; he was searching, searching for a peace that eluded him, a release from the memory that haunted his every step.

The Serpent's Strike

He tracked a magnificent stag, its antlers like a crown of the forest, when a twig snapped behind him. A shiver ran down his spine, a primal unease. He whirled around, but too late. A dark arrow, fletched with feathers as black as night, slammed into his shoulder. The stag vanished, forgotten. Pain, sharp and searing, ignited his senses, but it was overshadowed by a white-hot rage. This was no accident. This was deliberate.

A Desperate Chase

Arjun roared, a sound of pure fury that echoed through the trees. He stumbled, his breath catching in his throat, but the burning desire for vengeance propelled him forward. He glimpsed a shadowy figure weaving through the dense undergrowth, mocking him with its swiftness. "I'll find you!" he screamed, his voice raw. "I'll make you pay!" Thorns tore at his clothes, branches clawed at his face, but he pressed on, driven by a primal need for retribution. The forest, once his sanctuary, now felt like a prison, trapping him in a cycle of pain and anger.

The Sanctuary of Silence

His quarry was gone, swallowed by the forest's depths. Arjun collapsed by a stream, his strength finally giving way. The arrow throbbed in his shoulder, each pulse a reminder of his vulnerability. He ripped at the fletching, trying to dislodge the arrow, but agony lanced through him, forcing him to stop. He was trapped, both physically and emotionally.

Suddenly, a presence made itself known. An old hermit, his eyes like pools of ancient wisdom, stood silently watching him. There was no judgment in his gaze, only a profound understanding.

"Vengeance will not heal you, young hunter," the hermit said, his voice soft but firm.

Arjun scoffed. "He attacked me! He deserves to suffer!"

"And will his suffering mend your wound?" the hermit countered. "Will it bring back what you've lost?"

The Weight of the Arrow

Arjun fell silent, the hermit's words hitting their mark. He looked at the arrow, at the blood staining his hand, and a chilling realization washed over him. He was so consumed by anger, by the desire for revenge, that he had forgotten the pain itself.

"This arrow," the hermit continued, "is but a symbol. We all carry arrows within us – the arrows of betrayal, the arrows of regret, the arrows of fear. The past is an arrow already flown. To chase it is to wound yourself anew. Wisdom lies not in retrieving the arrow, but in learning from its flight."

The Path to Healing

The hermit knelt beside Arjun, his touch gentle. He examined the wound, his movements deft and sure. "Let me help you," he said.

Arjun, his rage finally spent, nodded. As the hermit tended to his wound, Arjun felt a strange sense of calm descend upon him. It wasn't just the physical pain that was subsiding; it was the weight of the past, the burden of his anger, that was finally lifting.

The Hermit's Sanctuary

The hermit's dwelling wasn't a crude hut as Arjun had imagined. It was a small, natural cave, its entrance hidden behind a curtain of cascading vines. Inside, the cave opened into a surprisingly spacious chamber. Smooth, moss-covered stones served as furniture. A small fire crackled in a hearth built of river stones, casting a warm glow on the walls. Dried herbs hung from the cave ceiling, their fragrant aroma filling the air. A woven mat of reeds lay near the fire, and a collection of smooth, polished stones sat on a shelf carved into the rock. Arjun noticed a small, hand-carved wooden flute resting among the stones. The cave felt less like a refuge and more like a sanctuary, a place of peace and contemplation. It spoke of a life lived in harmony with nature, a life of simplicity and wisdom.

The Shadow of Doubt

As the hermit tended to his wound, Arjun's mind raced. He thought of his father, of the laughter that had been silenced by a single arrow. He thought of the years he had spent consumed by anger, by the burning desire to avenge his father's death. Had it all been for nothing? Had he wasted his life chasing a ghost, a shadow of the past? The hermit's words echoed in his mind: "The past is an arrow already flown..." Was it true? Could he truly let go of his anger, his pain? Doubt gnawed at him, a cold serpent in his heart.

The Balm of Acceptance

The hermit's touch was gentle, his movements precise. He cleansed Arjun's wound with a mixture of herbs and spring water, his touch surprisingly light despite the strength evident in his weathered hands. As he applied a poultice of crushed leaves to the wound, a soothing warmth spread through Arjun's shoulder, easing not only the physical pain but also the ache in his heart. The hermit worked in silence, his focus absolute, his presence a calming balm in the storm of Arjun's emotions.

The Language of Silence

Days passed in the quiet sanctuary of the hermit's cave. Arjun learned the rhythm of the forest, the subtle language of rustling leaves, the whispers of the wind. He observed the hermit's daily routine – the gathering of herbs, the tending of the fire, the quiet contemplation of the setting sun. The hermit spoke little, but his silence was eloquent, filled with a wisdom that transcended words. Arjun began to understand that true communication wasn't just about speaking; it was about listening, not just with the ears, but with the heart.

The Weight of the Past, the Hope of the Future

As his wound healed, so too did Arjun's spirit. The weight of the past, the burden of his anger, began to lighten. He realized that his father wouldn't want him to live a life consumed by vengeance. He would want him to live, to learn, to grow. The hermit's words echoed in his mind: "The past is an arrow already flown. To chase it is to wound yourself anew. Wisdom lies not in retrieving the arrow, but in learning from its flight." Arjun finally understood. He couldn't change the past, but he could choose how he would respond to it. He could choose healing over hatred, forgiveness over vengeance.

The Return

The day came when Arjun knew it was time to return to his village. He thanked the hermit for his kindness and his wisdom. "Remember," the hermit said, his eyes twinkling, "the forest gives and the forest takes. But it also teaches. Learn from its lessons, and you will find your path." Arjun emerged from the forest a changed man. His physical wound was healed, but more importantly, his emotional wounds were mending. He walked with a new sense of purpose, a quiet strength that radiated from within.

A New Kind of Hunter

Arjun's return was met with joy and relief. His fellow villagers had feared the worst. But they soon realized that he was no longer just a skilled hunter. He had become a wise man, a counselor, a guide. He shared the lessons he had learned in the forest, the wisdom he had gained from the hermit. He taught them that true strength wasn't about physical prowess or the ability to wield a bow. It was about resilience, about compassion, about the courage to heal and move forward.

The Legacy of the Arrow

Arjun continued to hunt, providing for his village, but his focus had shifted. He no longer sought just animals; he sought understanding. He listened to the villagers' problems, their fears, their sorrows. He shared his own story, the story of the arrow, not as a tale of vengeance, but as a parable of healing. He showed them that even the deepest wounds could be mended, that even the darkest past could be overcome. And in doing so, he found his own peace, one healed heart at a time.

Moral of the Story:

"The past holds valuable lessons, but dwelling on it only prolongs the pain. True strength lies in healing, forgiveness, and using our experiences to guide ourselves and others toward a better future. We can choose to be defined by our wounds or by our resilience. The choice is ours."

II

The Greedy Shadow

*"The hunger for more often blinds us to the
abundance we already possess."*

The Glittering Deception

In the tranquil village of Kambakam, nestled amidst emerald fields and swaying coconut palms, lived a farmer named Sundaram. His life was a symphony of simple pleasures – the warmth of the sun on his skin, the laughter of his children, the quiet satisfaction of a bountiful harvest. His small plot of land provided enough, his family was loving, and his heart was content. "Enough is plenty," he often said, a philosophy that guided his life.

The Whisper of Gold

One evening, as the sun dipped below the horizon, painting the sky in hues of orange and purple, Sundaram stumbled upon something glittering in his field. He knelt, his fingers brushing against the cool earth, and unearthed a golden coin. Intrigued, he dug further, and his heart pounded with a mixture of excitement and disbelief as he unearthed a pot filled with gold coins. A treasure! A gift from the gods, he thought.

The Seed of Greed

At first, Sundaram used his newfound wealth wisely. He expanded his farm, purchased better tools, and even built a small school for the village children. He was hailed as a benefactor, a generous and wise man. But as the villagers sang his praises, a subtle shift began to occur within him. The gold, once a symbol of opportunity, began to whisper insidious suggestions in his dreams. "Why stop here?" it murmured. "You could own the entire village. You could be the richest man in the region."

The Shadow Grows

The seed of greed, once dormant, began to sprout and grow within Sundaram's heart. He started acquiring more land, hiring more workers, and amassing wealth beyond his wildest dreams. The more he gained, the more he craved. His peaceful nights were replaced by restless anxieties. "What if someone steals my gold?" he worried. "What if I lose everything?" The shadow of his greed grew larger, darkening his once bright spirit.

The Price of Ambition

His family, once the center of his world, became a mere distraction. His fields, once a source of joy and fulfillment, were now just tools for generating more profit. He lost sight of the simple pleasures that had once brought him so much happiness. He even cut down the villagers' beloved mango grove to make way for yet another warehouse, sacrificing community goodwill for the relentless pursuit of wealth.

The Sage's Mirror

One day, as Sundaram paced anxiously in front of his grand mansion, an old sage named Jnanananda passed through the village. He observed Sundaram's troubled countenance and approached him gently. "You seem burdened, my son," Jnanananda said.

Sundaram scoffed. "Burdened? I am the wealthiest man in Kambakam. What burden could I possibly have?"

Jnanananda smiled knowingly. "Wealth is like fire," he said, his voice soft but firm. "When it warms you, it is a blessing. But when it burns uncontrollably, it consumes everything in its path. Tell me, Sundaram, are you truly happy?"

Sundaram froze. He hadn't smiled in months. The weight of his wealth had become a suffocating burden, a prison of his own making. "Wise one," he pleaded, "what must I do?"

Jnanananda handed him a small, polished mirror. "Look into this each day," he advised. "See if the man you have become is one you admire. If not, then let go of the excess, for it is not your wealth that haunts you, but your own shadow."

The Reflection of Truth

That night, Sundaram stared into the mirror. He saw a man with tired, haunted eyes, a man consumed by anxiety and greed. The image of his former self – the joyful farmer who cherished simple moments – flashed before him, a stark contrast to the man he had become. Overwhelmed with regret, he made a decision.

The Dawn of Redemption

The next morning, Sundaram gathered the villagers. He stood before them, his voice trembling but firm. "I have allowed greed to consume me," he confessed. "I have forgotten the true meaning of happiness. I will return the land I have taken, I will replant the mango grove, and I will use my wealth to benefit us all."

As Sundaram shared his wealth and restored balance to the village, the shadow of greed began to recede from his life. The restless whispers that had tormented him disappeared, replaced by the genuine laughter of his family and the heartfelt gratitude of his people.

The True Treasure

Sundaram learned a valuable lesson: Wealth is a tool, not a master. When used with wisdom and compassion, it can bring peace and prosperity. But when worshipped blindly, it becomes a dark shadow that consumes all light. Kambakam flourished once more, not under the oppressive weight of riches, but under the radiant glow of shared prosperity and contentment. Sundaram had finally discovered the true treasure – not gold, but the wisdom to use it for the good of all.

Moral of the story:

"*True wealth is found in the balance of contentment, compassion, and shared prosperity, not just in material possessions.*"

III

The Mirror of Incompatible Reflections

"The truest reflection is not what we see in the mirror, but what we create in the world."

The Duality of Dreams

In a town nestled amidst the embrace of emerald hills, two individuals, Sundaram and Chandrika, stood as testaments to the diverse tapestry of human potential. Sundaram, a scientist whose mind was a crucible of innovation, forged inventions that reshaped the world around him. His name echoed through the halls of academia and industry, a symbol of progress and ingenuity. Chandrika, an artist whose soul found expression in a symphony ofcolors, painted emotions that resonated with the deepest chambers of the human heart. Yet, despite their shared brilliance, Chandrika felt her own light dimmed by the radiant glow of Sundaram's achievements.

The Whispers of Inadequacy

Chandrika admired Sundaram, recognizing the profound impact of his work. But a quiet whisper of inadequacy echoed within her own soul. Every accolade bestowed upon Sundaram felt like a subtle reminder of her own perceived insignificance. "Sundaram is changing the world," she would muse, her voice tinged with a hint of melancholy, "while I merely create images that adorn walls, fleeting glimpses of beauty in a world often too busy to notice." Trapped in the labyrinth of comparison, Chandrika convinced herself that her contributions were but pale shadows compared to the tangible advancements of Sundaram's inventions.

The Sanctuary of the Banyan Tree

One day, seeking respite from the gnawing whispers of self-doubt, Chandrika sought solace in the tranquil embrace of the surrounding forest. The dappled sunlight filtering through the leaves, the gentle murmur of the wind, the earthy scent of the forest floor – all these offered a momentary balm to her troubled spirit. Beneath the sprawling canopy of an ancient banyan tree, she encountered an old hermit, Jnanananda, his eyes deep pools of wisdom. Observing her troubled countenance, Jnanananda inquired, "Why do you carry such a heavy heart, child?" **The Burden of Comparison** Chandrika, hesitant at first, eventually poured out her feelings of inadequacy. "I feel so insignificant," she confessed, her voice barely a whisper. "Sundaram is a genius, celebrated by all. He makes a tangible difference in the world. What value do my paintings hold compared to his groundbreaking inventions?"

The Mirror of Self

Jnanananda listened patiently, his gaze filled with gentle understanding. "Come with me," he said, his voice soft yet firm, leading Chandrika deeper into the heart of the forest. They arrived at an ancient hall, its walls lined with mirrors of every conceivable shape and size, each crafted from a different material, each reflecting light in a unique way. "Stand before these mirrors," Jnanananda instructed, "and you will not see your outward reflection, but the essence of who you truly are."

The Tapestry of Talent

Intrigued, Chandrika approached the first mirror, a shimmering expanse of polished silver. To her astonishment, it did not reflect her familiar image. Instead, it revealed a vision of a child, radiant with joy, clutching a vibrant painting, her eyes sparkling with unbridled creativity. "This," Jnanananda explained, "is the joy you bring to the hearts of those who behold your art. You capture the fleeting beauty of a moment and make iteternal." The second mirror, crafted from smoky quartz, revealed a barren room transformed into a sanctuary of color and life, pulsating with energy and beauty. "This," Jnanananda continued, "is the vibrancy you infuse into the world. Without your colors, Chandrika, life would be a canvas devoid of light, a symphony without music." The third mirror, made of clear crystal, reflected Chandrika comforting a grieving friend with words of solace and compassion, her touch gentle and reassuring. "And this," Jnanananda added, "is your unique ability to touch lives in ways that transcend the power of invention. You offer comfort, you inspire hope, you remind us of our shared humanity." The Symphony of Self-Acceptance As Chandrika moved from mirror to mirror, she witnessed a kaleidoscope of her own being – her creativity, her empathy, her singular perspective. Each reflection unveiled a facet of her essence that she had, in her self-doubt, overlooked. "Do you see now?" Jnanananda asked gently. "You are not meant to be Sundaram, just as Sundaram is not meant to be you. His inventions may reshape the physical world, but your art reshapes hearts. Both are equally vital, equally precious, equally necessary for the flourishing of the human spirit." Tears welled in Chandrika's eyes, tears of understanding, of acceptance, of liberation. She had spent so long measuring herself against another's yardstick that she had forgotten to recognize her own inherent worth, her own unique contribution to the world. "Thank you," she whispered, her voice filled with gratitude, bowing deeply to Jnanananda.

The Dance of Creation

Returning to the town, Chandrika felt a lightness she hadn't experienced in years. The burden of comparison had finally lifted, replaced by a profound sense of self-acceptance. She no longer saw Sundaram as a rival, but as a fellow artist, a fellow creator, each contributing their unique brushstrokes to the grand canvas of human expression. Sundaram, noticing the newfound confidence radiating from Chandrika, approached her one day, his eyes filled with genuine admiration. "Your recent mural in the town square," he remarked, his voice filled with genuine appreciation, "it moved me profoundly. It made me pause and truly see the beauty that surrounds us, the beauty we so often overlook in our daily lives. I may create inventions, Chandrika, but your art gives meaning to the world in which we live, it gives voice to the unspoken emotions that connect us all."

The Harmony of Gifts

From that moment on, Sundaram and Chandrika became mutual admirers, recognizing the equal significance of their distinct contributions. Chandrika no longer saw Sundaram as a rival, but as a reminder that each individual possesses a unique and invaluable role to play in the grand tapestry of existence, that the world needs both the logic of science and the beauty of art, both the power of invention and the solace of expression.

Moral of the story:

*"Just as a symphony requires both the strings and the woodwinds,
the world needs both science and art, innovation and expression.
Embrace your unique gifts, for your value lies not in comparison, but
in the distinct melody you bring to the harmony of life."*

IV

The Awakening

*"The greatest awakening is realizing that the
treasures we seek outside ourselves are often hidden
within."*

The Price of Ambition

Karthik was a man driven by a singular mantra: success above all else.
Born into a family of modest means, he had witnessed firsthand the harsh
realities of poverty and vowed to never let it define his destiny. Through
relentless hard work, shrewd business acumen, and a willingness to bend
the rules, he built a thriving empire, his name synonymous with wealth
and achievement. But in his relentless pursuit of material success, Karthik
sacrificed the very things that truly mattered – his relationships, his family,
and his own happiness.

His wife, Meera, once a source of unwavering support and infectious
laughter, found herself increasingly neglected. "Karthik," she would plead,
her voice heavy with concern, "our children barely know you. They yearn for
your presence, for your love." But Karthik, blinded by his ambition, would
brush aside her concerns. "I'm doing this for all of you," he would retort,
"sacrifices must be made."

The Crumbling Facade

Time, relentless and unforgiving, marched on. Meera, weary of empty promises and a husband perpetually absent in spirit, reached her breaking point. One evening, Karthik returned home to find a note on the otherwise empty dining table. "Karthik," it read, "I've waited patiently for you to come home, not just physically, but emotionally. But you're always elsewhere, chasing a dream I no longer recognize. I'm taking the children to my parents' house. Perhaps there, we can find the love that has vanished from our home."

A pang of regret flickered in Karthik's heart, but he quickly extinguished it with the cold logic of ambition. "She'll understand eventually," he muttered to himself, burying his emotions beneath a mountain of work.

Years turned into a blur of business deals, acquisitions, and ruthless strategies. Karthik honed his skills, becoming a master manipulator, a shrewd tactician who thought nothing of crushing his competitors, even resorting to unethical means to maintain his position at the top. "Business is war," he rationalized, ignoring the trail of broken trust and severed relationships he left in his wake.

The Scales of Karma

But karma, as it often does, had a way of balancing the scales. One day, Rajan, Karthik's most trusted business partner, betrayed him, exposing his shady dealings to the world. Clients withdrew their support, lawsuits piled up, and Karthik's once-impregnable empire began to crumble like a sandcastle in a rising tide.

Desperate, Karthik reached out to his family, but Meera, her heart wounded and her trust shattered, refused to answer his calls. His children, now teenagers, had grown distant, their memories of their father clouded by years of neglect. Even his friends, once readily available, had moved on, their patience exhausted by his self-absorption.

The Mirror of Truth

One day, Ravi, a friend from Karthik's past, paid him a visit. "I heard what happened," Ravi said gently. Karthik, overwhelmed by a torrent of emotions he had long suppressed, confessed, "Ravi, I've lost everything. My family, my friends, my reputation... there's nothing left."

Ravi listened patiently, his gaze steady and compassionate. "You've built walls so high around yourself, Karthik," he observed, "that no one could climb them. People tried to reach you, but you never let them in. Life isn't just about what you gain; it's about who you share it with."

Ravi's words struck a chord deep within Karthik's soul. He began to see the cracks in the foundation of his life, the emptiness beneath the veneer of success. But just as he resolved to make amends, fate dealt him a final, devastating blow. Karthik was diagnosed with a terminal illness.

The Reckoning

Alone and confined to his bed, Karthik embarked on a painful journey of introspection. He reflected on his life, the choices he had made, the relationships he had sacrificed, and the love he had squandered. He poured out his heart in a letter, a testament to his regrets and a plea for forgiveness.

"To those I have hurt, abandoned, or neglected," he wrote, "I am truly sorry. I understand now that life is not measured by wealth or power, but by the love we share and the connections we nurture. I broke hearts, severed ties, and traded moments of joy for fleeting triumphs. I wish I could undo the past, but all I can do is implore you to cherish the people in your life before it's too late. Live with love, not ambition. Forgive me for realizing this only at the precipice of my own demise."

The Legacy of Regret

When Karthik passed away, his letter was shared far and wide, touching the hearts of those who read it. Meera and their children wept for the man who had finally awakened to the true cost of his choices. His story became a cautionary tale, a poignant reminder to prioritize love, kindness, and connection above the allure of ambition.

Moral of the story:

"True wealth lies not in what we accumulate, but in who we share our lives with. Let love, not ambition, be your guiding star, for in the end, it is the bonds we forge and the hearts we touch that truly define

our legacy."

&

V

The Silent Observer

*"The loudest voice is not always the strongest.
Sometimes, the greatest power lies in quiet
observation."*

The Storm Within

In a quaint village nestled amidst rolling hills, lived a young woman named
Nila. Her spirit, like the fiery chilies that grew in her garden, was quick
to ignite, her words as sharp as the thorns on the acacia trees that lined
the village paths. Nila was known for her outspoken nature, her honesty
as blunt as the village blacksmith's hammer. If someone wronged her or
crossed a line, she would not hesitate to confront them, her voice ringing
out like a temple bell, summoning attention to injustice. While her courage
was admired, her confrontational nature often left her feeling drained and
isolated, her relationships strained by the constant friction.

The Sting of Betrayal

One day, during the vibrant celebration of the village festival, Nila overheard
a conversation that pierced her heart like a poisoned arrow. Two of her
closest friends, their voices hushed but their words as venomous as cobras,

were gossiping about her. They mocked her straightforwardness, her quick temper, and the way she seemed to keep others at bay. Hurt and anger surged through Nila, a tempest threatening to consume her.

Unable to bear the sting of betrayal, Nila stormed towards her friends, her eyes blazing with fury. A heated confrontation ensued, their voices rising above the festive music and laughter, drawing the attention of the entire village. Though Nila felt a momentary sense of vindication, she soon realized the cost of her outburst. In the days that followed, people began to avoid her, their smiles strained, their conversations guarded. The isolation she had always feared deepened, her fiery spirit now a flickering flame in the cold wind of rejection.

The Wisdom of the Banyan Tree

Seeking solace and guidance, Nila visited her grandmother, Anjamma, a woman whose wisdom was as deep as the village well, her spirit as serene as the moonlit sky. Anjamma listened patiently as Nila recounted her woes, her voice trembling with hurt and frustration. Then, taking Nila by the hand, she led her to the garden behind their home.

Anjamma pointed to a majestic banyan tree, its branches reaching towards the heavens, its leaves rustling gently in the breeze. "Do you see how the tree does not fight the wind, my child?" she asked. "It sways silently, gracefully, allowing the wind to pass through its leaves without resistance. That is how it grows strong, without breaking."

Nila, her brow furrowed in confusion, looked at her grandmother. "But Grandmaa," she questioned, "what if the wind is too harsh? What if it threatens to damage the tree?"

Anjamma smiled, her eyes twinkling with wisdom. "The tree does not confront the wind with anger or resistance," she explained. "It sets boundaries by growing deeper roots, by strengthening its bark. It learns from the seasons, adapting silently, patiently. You too, my child, must learn to observe and adapt. Not every offense requires a battle. Sometimes, silence and boundaries are more powerful than words."

The Power of Silent Observation

Nila spent the following weeks pondering her grandmother's words, her fiery spirit slowly cooling, replaced by a growing sense of self-awareness.

She began to observe the people around her, their actions, their words, their intentions, instead of reacting impulsively. When she noticed someone being insincere or disrespectful, she didn't confront them with her usual fiery passion. Instead, she quietly distanced herself, focusing on nurturing relationships with those who genuinely valued her, those whose spirits resonated with her own.

The Transformation

Over time, a remarkable transformation took place. Nila's inner turmoil subsided, replaced by a newfound calmness. Her relationships deepened, built on a foundation of mutual respect and understanding. Her presence, once associated with fiery outbursts, now commanded a quiet respect, a recognition of her inner strength and wisdom. People were drawn to her newfound serenity, seeking her company and her counsel.

One day, a young girl from the village approached Nila, her eyes wide with admiration. "How do you stay so calm when people hurt you?" she asked.

Nila smiled gently, her gaze filled with understanding. "Maturity has taught me that I don't need to confront every wrong," she replied. "I observe, I understand, and I set my boundaries. That is all the strength I need."

Moral of the story:

"True strength lies not in the force of our reactions, but in the wisdom of our responses. Silence, coupled with observation and clear boundaries, can be a powerful tool for navigating the complexities of human interaction."

VI

The Unbreakable Bond

*"True friendship is a shelter that can withstand the
fiercest storms of life."*

The Seed of a Promise

In the village of Vrindavan, where the air was sweet with the scent of
jasmine and the ancient banyan trees cast long, cool shadows, two
childhood friends, Radha and Krishna, shared a bond as resilient as the
roots that intertwined beneath their favorite banyan tree. Their laughter
echoed through the sun-dappled groves, their secrets whispered in the
twilight's embrace, their dreams woven into the fabric of their shared
experiences. They made a promise, a childhood vow to remain forever
connected, their friendship a constant in the ever-changing tapestry of life.

Years passed, and the carefree days of childhood gave way to the
responsibilities of adulthood. Radha's family moved to a distant city, leaving
Krishna behind to tend to his family's farm in Vrindavan. Though miles
separated them, their hearts remained intertwined, their bond nurtured
by letters filled with shared memories and the lingering warmth of their
childhood connection.

The Winds of Change

One day, a ferocious storm descended upon Vrindavan, its fury unleashing torrential rains and howling winds that threatened to tear the village asunder. News of the storm reached Radha's family, their hearts heavy with worry for Krishna's safety. They embarked on a perilous journey back to Vrindavan, their every step fueled by a desperate hope that their beloved friend had weathered the storm.

Upon their arrival, they found the village in ruins. Homes were reduced to rubble, fields were submerged beneath a raging torrent, and the once-vibrant community was cloaked in a veil of despair. Radha's heart pounded with a mixture of fear and determination as she searched for Krishna amidst the wreckage. Finally, she found him near the ancient banyan tree, its branches battered but its trunk still standing tall, a symbol of resilience in the face of devastation.

The Banyan's Embrace

Krishna, though injured and shaken, was alive. He had sought shelter beneath the banyan tree, its sturdy trunk and sprawling canopy providing a sanctuary from the storm's wrath. As Radha rushed towards him, tears of relief blurring her vision, she noticed something profound. The banyan tree, a silent observer of their childhood promise, had shielded Krishna from harm, its roots anchoring him to the earth, its branches protecting him from the elements.

In that moment, the true meaning of their bond resonated deep within Radha's soul. It wasn't just a childhood vow; it was a connection woven into the very fabric of their beings, a tapestry of shared experiences, unspoken understanding, and unwavering support. It was a bond that had withstood the test of time and distance, a testament to the enduring power of true friendship.

The Healing

Together, Radha and Krishna joined the villagers in the arduous task of rebuilding their homes and their lives. Their unbreakable bond, forged in childhood and strengthened by the shared experience of the storm, became a beacon of hope for the entire community. It reminded them that even in the darkest of times, love and friendship could provide the strength, resilience, and unwavering support needed to overcome adversity.

Moral of the story:

"True friendship is an unbreakable bond that can withstand the fiercest storms of life. Nurture your friendships, for they are the anchors that keep you grounded, the shelters that protect you, and the guiding stars that lead you through the darkest nights."

VII

The Banyan Bond

"The strongest bonds are forged not in the fires of celebration, but in the crucible of shared hardship."

Whispers of Doubt

In the sun-drenched village of Govindapuram, nestled amidst the verdant hills of South India, life flowed at the gentle pace of grazing cattle and the rhythmic chants of ancient traditions. The Yadav community, known for their unwavering devotion to Lord Krishna and their sacred cows, formed the backbone of the village, their lives intertwined with the rhythms of the land and the cycles of nature.

Among them was Gauri, a young woman whose spirit shone as bright as the morning sun, yet whose heart carried the weight of a profound loss. Married at a tender age, she had known the joys of companionship and the promise of a future filled with love and laughter. But fate, in its cruel capriciousness, had snatched away her happiness, leaving her a widow with a young son to care for and a legacy of whispers and pity to endure.

"She is cursed," the villagers muttered, their voices laced with superstition and fear. "What future can she possibly have now?"

The Strength Within

But Gauri, though wounded by grief, refused to surrender to despair. She rose with the dawn each day, her spirit as resilient as the banyan tree that stood sentinel at the village center. She tended to Nandini, her late husband's prized cow, her hands calloused but her movements gentle. She churned butter, the rhythmic motion a soothing balm for her troubled soul. And she delivered milk to the nearby temple, a small act of devotion that connected her to her husband's memory and provided sustenance for her son.

Yet, as the months turned into seasons, the whispers grew louder, the stares more judgmental. Gauri found herself increasingly isolated, a solitary figure navigating a landscape of sorrow and suspicion.

A Helping Hand

One evening, as Gauri struggled to repair a broken fence that separated her small pasture from the village fields, a familiar voice broke through her solitude. It was Kannan, a young Yadav man known for his skill in training cattle and his gentle spirit. Kannan and Gauri had shared a carefree childhood, their laughter echoing through the banyan groves, their dreams woven into the fabric of their shared experiences. Though their paths had diverged in adulthood, Kannan had always admired Gauri's resilience, her unwavering determination in the face of adversity.

"Let me help you," Kannan offered, his voice kind and steady.

Gauri, her pride wounded and her spirit weary, snapped back, "I don't need your help."

But Kannan, sensing her vulnerability beneath the facade of strength, did not waver. He stayed by her side, mending the fence in silence, his presence a quiet testament to his unwavering support. When the work was done, he spoke softly, his words carrying the weight of understanding. "It's okay to need help, Gauri. Even the strongest among us lean on others sometimes."

The Banyan's Witness

Kannan's presence became a source of comfort and strength for Gauri. He helped her rebuild the shed for Nandini, sharing his knowledge of carpentry and cattle care. He taught her son how to train the calves, his laughter mingling with the boy's as they worked side-by-side. And he brought fodder during the lean seasons, ensuring that Nandini remained healthy and strong.

But their growing connection did not go unnoticed by the villagers. Whispers turned into murmurs, and murmurs into accusations. "Why is Kannan always at her house?" they gossiped. "A widow and a young man... it's improper."

The weight of judgment threatened to crush Gauri's spirit. One evening, unable to bear the burden any longer, she confronted Kannan beneath the sprawling banyan tree that stood at the heart of the village. The banyan, a silent witness to generations of joys and sorrows, was where the community gathered for festivals and disputes. But tonight, it was a sanctuary for two souls seeking solace and understanding.

"Why are you doing this?" Gauri asked, her voice trembling with a mixture of frustration and fear. "Don't you care what people say about us? About you?"

Kannan looked at her, his gaze steady and unwavering. "Let them talk," he said. "They don't know your strength, your struggles. I've seen the worst of your days, Gauri, and I've stayed because I believe in the best of you. That's what matters to me."

The Strength of Shared Burdens

Kannan's words pierced through Gauri's defenses, melting the icy armor she had built around her heart. For so long, she had fought her battles alone, convinced that strength meant keeping everyone at bay. But Kannan's unwavering support, his willingness to stand by her side despite the whispers and judgments, revealed a different kind of strength – the strength to allow others in, to share burdens, and to build a future together.

Months later, during the joyous celebration of Gopashtami, the festival honoring Lord Krishna and the sacred cows, Gauri and Kannan unveiled their shared vision – a new dairy collective that would benefit the entire Yadav community. Gauri's dedication to her craft, combined with Kannan's expertise in cattle training, created a model of resilience, cooperation, and shared prosperity.

The village elders, moved by their initiative and their unwavering commitment to the community, blessed their endeavor. "The banyan tree has witnessed generations of bonds," one elder proclaimed. "Today, it witnesses a bond built on trust, respect, and devotion to our heritage. May it inspire us all."

A Legacy of Resilience

Years passed, and the story of Gauri and Kannan became a cherished tale whispered beneath the banyan tree, a testament to the enduring power of friendship, loyalty, and shared purpose. It was a reminder that the strongest bonds are forged not in the fires of celebration, but in the crucible of shared hardship, where those who see us at our worst choose to stay, offering a hand, a shoulder, and a steadfast heart.

Moral of the story:

"True strength lies not in facing life's challenges alone, but in allowing the right people to stand by your side. Those who see you at your worst and choose to stay are the ones who truly deserve to be part of your best. Loyalty, trust, and mutual respect can overcome even the harshest judgments of society, leading to resilience, growth, and meaningful bonds that stand the test of time."

VIII

The Wealth of Integrity

"Integrity is a seed that blossoms into a harvest of trust, respect, and enduring wealth."

The Seeds of Contentment

In the heart of Thanjavur, a village where the emerald paddy fields stretched towards the horizon and the majestic Brihadeeswara Temple cast its long shadow, lived Raghunandan, a farmer whose heart was as fertile as the land he tilled. Though his plot was small and his dwelling modest, Raghunandan possessed a wealth that could not be measured in gold or grain – the wealth of integrity, kindness, and an unwavering commitment to his community.

His days unfolded in a rhythm as ancient as the temple itself. He would rise with the dawn, offering prayers of gratitude for the blessings of the earth and the bounty of the harvest. He would share a portion of his yield with those less fortunate, his generosity a quiet testament to his belief in the interconnectedness of all beings. And in the evenings, beneath the sprawling canopy of the village banyan tree, he would gather the children, their laughter mingling with the rustling leaves as he shared stories and imparted wisdom.

The Arrogance of Wealth

While others in the village chased after material riches, their ambitions fueled by a desire for status and power, Raghunandan found contentment in the simple pleasures of life – the warmth of the sun on his skin, the laughter of children, and the satisfaction of contributing to the well-being of his community. He measured his success not by the size of his granary, but by the smiles he brought to the faces of those around him.

Among the wealthy men of Thanjavur, Muthu Pillai stood out as a paragon of arrogance and greed. He owned the largest rice mill in the region, his coffers overflowing with the profits extracted from the labor of others. He scoffed at Raghunandan's simple ways, his disdain evident in every encounter. "What use is honesty," he would sneer, "if it doesn't fill your pockets?"

The Crucible of Drought

Fate, however, had a way of testing the true measure of a man. A devastating drought descended upon Thanjavur, its relentless grip turning the once-lush paddy fields into arid wastelands. Despair cast a long shadow over the village, and hunger gnawed at the bellies of its people.

Muthu Pillai, ever opportunistic, saw the drought as a chance to further increase his wealth. He raised the price of grain to exorbitant levels, forcing many villagers to sell their land and their livelihoods just to survive. His greed knew no bounds, his heart hardened by the pursuit of profit.

The Abundance of Integrity

Raghunandan, though facing his own struggles, refused to succumb to despair. He opened his small granary to those in need, sharing his meager reserves with unwavering generosity. "Hunger doesn't discriminate between rich and poor," he told his wife, Parvathi, as they distributed rice to a group of hungry children. "It only sees kindness."

Word of Raghunandan's selflessness spread like wildfire through the parched fields of Thanjavur. Villagers, their hopes rekindled by his compassion, flocked to him for help. He lent them grain, asking for nothing in return but a simple promise: "Repay me when the rains return."

Some scoffed at his naiveté, predicting his ruin. But Raghunandan remained steadfast, his faith in human goodness unshaken. "Wealth comes and goes," he would say, "but integrity stays."

The Harvest of Trust

Muthu Pillai, witnessing the growing respect for Raghunandan, seethed with envy. "Your charity will be your downfall," he warned. "Mark my words, when the drought returns, you will be left with nothing."

But Raghunandan, his eyes fixed on the horizon of hope, replied calmly, "Wealth nourishes the body, Pillai, but integrity nourishes the soul."

Months crawled by, each day a test of endurance. Then, finally, the skies opened, and the life-giving rains returned to Thanjavur. The villagers, their hearts overflowing with gratitude for Raghunandan's selfless generosity, rallied together to help him replant his fields. Even those who had borrowed from him repaid their debts, not just in grain, but in loyalty and friendship.

Raghunandan's small patch of land flourished, yielding a bountiful harvest that became a symbol of hope and resilience for the entire village. His integrity had not only sustained him through the drought but had also sown the seeds of trust and cooperation that would nourish the community for generations to come.

The True Measure of Wealth

One day, an elderly widow approached Raghunandan, her eyes filled with tears of gratitude. She offered him a small bag of rice, her voice trembling as she spoke. "This is all I can give," she said. "You saved my family from starvation."

Raghunandan smiled, his eyes twinkling with compassion. "Your gratitude is worth more than gold, Amma," he replied, gently placing his hand on her head. "Keep this for yourself."

As the years passed, Muthu Pillai's wealth brought him nothing but isolation and bitterness. His mansion, though grand, was devoid of warmth and laughter. His coffers, though overflowing, could not fill the emptiness in his heart.

Raghunandan, on the other hand, found himself surrounded by an abundance of love, respect, and genuine connection. His simple hut became a sanctuary for those seeking guidance and solace. His wisdom, rooted in integrity and compassion, became the foundation upon which the village thrived.

On his sixtieth birthday, the villagers gathered beneath the banyan tree to celebrate the man who had taught them the true meaning of greatness. One of the elders, his voice filled with admiration, proclaimed, "Raghunandan's wealth is not measured in coins or grains, but in the lives he has touched, the smiles he has brought, and the integrity with which he lives each day."

That evening, as the sun dipped below the horizon, painting the sky in hues of gold and crimson, Karthik, Raghunandan's son, sat beside his father, his eyes filled with wonder. "Appa," he asked, "will we ever be rich?"

Raghunandan looked at his son, his gaze filled with love and wisdom. "Kanna," he replied, "we are already rich. Rich in trust, in kindness, and in the love of those around us. Remember, the true measure of a man lies not in how much wealth he acquires, but in his ability to live with integrity and make a positive impact on the world. That is the greatest wealth of all."

Moral of the story:

"True wealth lies not in material possessions, but in the integrity with which we live our lives and the positive impact we have on others. Kindness, generosity, and an unwavering commitment to our values create a legacy that transcends any material riches."

౭౦

IX

The Unbroken Promise

"A promise to a child is a pledge to the future; a promise to a daughter is a commitment to change the world."

The Weight of Tradition

In the quiet village of Sevanapatti, nestled amidst the rolling hills and emerald paddy fields of Tamil Nadu, a deep-rooted tradition cast a long shadow over the lives of women. For generations, the birth of a girl child was met with a muted celebration, a bittersweet symphony of joy and sorrow. Sons were hailed as heirs, their arrival a cause for jubilant fanfare, while daughters were often seen as burdens, their futures clouded by the weight of societal expectations and the looming specter of dowry.

Thirupathi, a humble schoolteacher with a heart filled with compassion and a mind ignited by the ideals of equality, was determined to break this cycle of despair. He had witnessed the sorrow in his wife Lakshmi's eyes each time she overheard the whispers that followed the birth of their three daughters. "Another girl," the villagers would lament, their voices heavy with judgment. "How will they ever afford the dowries?"

Lakshmi, a daughter of the village herself, knew the silent curse that hung over the heads of girl children. But Thirupathi, her beloved husband, was different. He loved his daughters – Meera, Valli, and Kavya – with a fierce and unwavering devotion. To him, they were not liabilities, but blessings, their laughter the sweetest music, their dreams the brightest stars in his sky.

A Promise Made, A Promise Kept

When Lakshmi became pregnant for the fourth time, the pressure from relatives and neighbors intensified. "You need a son to carry forward your lineage," they insisted, their voices echoing the age-old prejudices that had shackled generations of women. They suggested a visit to a city clinic to determine the gender of the unborn child, their intentions veiled in a cloak of concern but their underlying message clear: a girl child was an unwelcome burden.

Thirupathi, however, stood firm, his resolve as unyielding as the ancient banyan tree that graced the village center. "A child is a gift from the gods," he declared, his voice ringing with conviction. "We will welcome whoever comes into our lives with open hearts and unwavering love."

Months later, a baby girl was born, her arrival a testament to Thirupathi's unwavering belief in the inherent worth of every child. They named her Ananya, meaning "unique," a name that reflected her individuality and the boundless potential that lay within her.

The Burden of Doubt

But the joy that filled Thirupathi and Lakshmi's home was met with a chilling indifference from many in the village. "Four daughters?" they scoffed. "How will you ever manage?"

Undeterred by the negativity, Thirupathi and Lakshmi made a solemn promise to themselves and to their daughters. They would create a world where their girls could dream without limits, where their aspirations would not be shackled by societal expectations or the weight of tradition. "We will educate them, no matter the cost," Thirupathi vowed, his voice filled with determination.

The Price of Progress

It was not an easy path. Thirupathi's modest teacher's salary barely covered their basic needs, but he worked tirelessly, tutoring children in the evenings and sacrificing his own comforts to ensure that his daughters received the best education possible. Lakshmi, ever resourceful, began weaving exquisite sarees, her nimble fingers transforming threads of silk into works of art that brought in much-needed income.

Dreams Take Flight

Years passed, and the girls flourished under the loving care and unwavering support of their parents. Meera, the eldest, blossomed into a brilliant mathematician, her mind a tapestry of numbers and equations. She won a state-level competition, earning a scholarship to a prestigious college, her achievements a testament to her intellectual prowess and her parents' unwavering belief in her potential.

Valli, with her deep connection to the land and her passion for sustainable living, discovered innovative ways to cultivate crops, earning the respect and admiration of even the most traditional village elders. Her experiments with organic farming and water conservation transformed the village landscape, her efforts a testament to her ingenuity and her commitment to preserving the earth for future generations.

Kavya, the quietest of the three, found her voice through art. Her paintings, vibrant and evocative, captured the essence of village life, the beauty of nature, and the depths of human emotion. Her work was displayed in a local art exhibition, her talent shining through the canvas, a testament to her creativity and her parents' unwavering support for her artistic pursuits.

And little Ananya, inspired by her sisters' achievements, declared with unwavering conviction, "I want to be a doctor and save lives." Her dream, though ambitious, was nurtured by her parents' unwavering belief in her potential.

The Seeds of Change

Thirupathi and Lakshmi's unwavering commitment to their daughters' education did not go unchallenged. Neighbors and relatives questioned their choices, their voices echoing the ingrained prejudices of generations past. "What's the use of educating girls?" they scoffed. "They'll just get married and leave anyway."

But Thirupathi, his voice calm but firm, would retort, "Their education is not for anyone else's benefit; it's for their own. Every child, regardless of gender, deserves the opportunity to learn, to grow, and to discover their own unique potential."

A Village Transformed

One day, a tragedy struck the neighboring village, a stark reminder of the consequences of neglecting women's health and education. A young woman, denied access to proper medical care during childbirth, lost her life, leaving behind a grieving family and a community in mourning.

Thirupathi, his heart heavy with sorrow, saw this tragedy as a turning point. He gathered the villagers beneath the banyan tree, its ancient branches casting a somber shadow over the gathering. With a voice filled with passion and conviction, he addressed the community.

"Do you see the price we pay for undervaluing our daughters?" he asked, his words echoing through the hushed crowd. "We deny them education, we deny them dreams, and in doing so, we deny ourselves a better future. Every girl deserves the chance to thrive, to become someone who can change the world. Let us not see them as burdens, but as the beacons of hope they truly are."

His words struck a chord, awakening a long-dormant sense of justice and compassion within the villagers. Slowly, but surely, change began to ripple through Sevanapatti. More girls enrolled in the local school, their laughter filling the classrooms, their minds eager to learn. Parents who had once dismissed education as unnecessary for girls began to dream big for their daughters, their aspirations fueled by Thirupathi's unwavering belief in the power of education to transform lives.

A Legacy of Hope

Years passed, and Thirupathi's daughters became beacons of inspiration for the entire village. Meera, the mathematician, used her skills to develop innovative solutions for local farmers, increasing their yields and improving their livelihoods. Valli, the agriculturalist, continued to champion sustainable farming practices, transforming Sevanapatti into a model of environmental consciousness. Kavya, the artist, used her paintings to raise awareness about social issues and inspire positive change. And Ananya, the aspiring doctor, pursued her medical studies with unwavering determination, her heart filled with a desire to serve her community and make a difference in the world.

On National Girl Child Day, the village gathered to celebrate Thirupathi's family, their achievements a testament to his unwavering commitment to empowering his daughters. Meera, now a successful data scientist, addressed the crowd, her voice filled with gratitude. "Our father taught us that dreams have no gender," she declared. "He didn't just give us life; he gave us the courage to live it fully."

Ananya, now a medical student, echoed her sister's sentiments. "Saving a girl child is not just about letting her be born," she emphasized. "It's about giving her the opportunity to live, to learn, and to make a difference in the world."

Thirupathi's journey was not just about raising his daughters; it was about transforming an entire village's mindset. His promise to empower his daughters and challenge the deeply ingrained prejudices against girl children had created a ripple effect, inspiring others to embrace change and create a more equitable future for all.

As the village women lit lamps in honor of National Girl Child Day, their flames illuminating the twilight sky, Thirupathi stood beside Lakshmi, his heart filled with pride and gratitude. He watched his daughters shine like the stars they were always meant to be, their brilliance a testament to the transformative power of love, education, and unwavering belief in the potential of every child.

Moral of the story:

"The true measure of a society's greatness lies in how it treats its daughters. Every girl child deserves the opportunity to dream, to thrive, and to fulfill her potential. By valuing and empowering our daughters, we not only uplift families but also build a brighter, more equitable future for all."

X

The Silent Thread

"When words fail, silence can be the most profound expression of love and support."

The Tapestry of Resilience

In the heart of Tamil Nadu's verdant countryside, where the gentle breeze carried the scent of jasmine and the rhythmic chirping of crickets filled the twilight hours, lay the village of Vallipuram. It was a place where life moved at a slower pace, where the bonds of community were as strong as the roots of the ancient banyan tree that shaded the village square, and where the kindness of its people was as abundant as the rice that grew in the surrounding fields.

Radha, a widow in her early forties, was the embodiment of resilience, her spirit a beacon of strength in the face of adversity. She had spent her life weaving a tapestry of love and devotion, caring for her family and nurturing her teenage son, Suriya. When her husband had passed away unexpectedly five years ago, Radha had shouldered the responsibilities of their small rice field, ensuring that Suriya's education continued uninterrupted. She was the pillar of her household, her unwavering determination a source of inspiration for all who knew her.

The Storm Within

But fate, it seemed, had another test in store for Radha. One evening, as the monsoon rains lashed against the village rooftops, tragedy struck once more. Suriya, returning from the nearby town on his bicycle, was involved in a devastating accident. A reckless driver, blinded by the downpour, had veered off the road, leaving Suriya with a fractured leg and a spirit shattered by the cruel twist of fate.

Suriya, a promising athlete with dreams of representing his state in running, found himself confined to his bed, his once-boundless energy replaced by a crushing despair. His laughter, which had once filled their home with joy, was silenced, replaced by a heart-wrenching silence that seemed to echo through the empty rooms.

Radha watched helplessly as her son retreated into a world of pain and isolation. She tried everything she could think of to reach him – comforting words, inspiring stories of athletes who had overcome adversity, and fervent prayers offered at the village temple. But nothing seemed to penetrate the wall of sorrow that Suriya had built around himself.

The Wisdom of Silence

One evening, as the rain continued its relentless assault on the village, Radha sat beside Suriya's bed, her hands weaving a garland of fragrant jasmine for the temple deity. Her elderly neighbor, Thatha, a retired schoolteacher known for his wisdom and his quiet empathy, shuffled into the room, his presence a comforting balm in the midst of their despair.

"Amma," Thatha said softly, lowering himself into the chair beside her, "you've done enough talking. Now, let silence speak."

Radha looked at him, her eyes filled with confusion. Thatha, sensing her bewilderment, continued, "Sometimes, what people need isn't advice or solutions. They need to know they're not alone in their pain. They need the comfort of silent companionship, the assurance that someone is there to share their burden without judgment or expectation."

The Unspoken Language of Love

The next morning, Radha made a quiet decision. She sat beside Suriya without uttering a word, her hands busy weaving the jasmine garland, just as she had every morning since his accident. She didn't try to force a conversation or offer empty platitudes. Instead, she simply sat, her presence a silent testament to her unwavering love and support.

Days turned into weeks, and the silence in their home deepened. But it was not an empty silence; it was a silence filled with the unspoken language of love, a language that transcended words and resonated deep within Suriya's wounded heart.

Radha continued her silent vigil, her actions speaking volumes. She brought him his favorite idli and coconut chutney, even when he refused to eat. She hummed the soft lullabies she used to sing when he was a child, their melodies filling the quiet room with a sense of comfort and familiarity. And she sat beside him in the evenings, her presence a constant, calming force in the midst of his inner turmoil.

The Healing Begins

One evening, as the golden light of the setting sun filtered through the window, casting a warm glow on Suriya's face, he finally spoke. "Amma," he said, his voice hoarse and filled with emotion, "what if I never run again? What if I'm not the same?"

Radha, her heart aching for her son's pain, placed her hand gently on his. "Suriya," she said, her voice soft but firm, "whether you run or not, you are my son. And you are more than just your legs. You are my pride, my joy, my everything."

Tears welled up in Suriya's eyes, and for the first time since the accident, he allowed himself to grieve, to release the pent-up emotions that had been weighing him down. Radha held him close, her touch speaking a language that words could never express.

As the weeks passed, Suriya's spirit began to heal. Inspired by his mother's quiet strength and unwavering support, he embarked on his physiotherapy sessions with renewed determination. His friends, who had once been kept at bay by his silence, returned, their laughter and camaraderie filling the once-quiet home with warmth and life.

The Unspoken Lesson

One day, Thatha came to visit, his eyes twinkling with wisdom. He observed Suriya's progress, his smile a testament to the healing power of silent companionship. "You see, Amma," he said to Radha, "your silence spoke volumes."

Months later, during the village's annual temple festival, Suriya surprised everyone by participating in the procession dance. Though he wasn't running yet, his steps were steady, his smile wide, and his heart filled with a newfound appreciation for the simple joys of life. The villagers cheered as Radha watched, her eyes brimming with pride and gratitude.

In Vallipuram, the story of Radha and Suriya became a quiet legend, a testament to the power of human connection and the unspoken language of love. It was a reminder that in our darkest moments, what we often need most is not advice or solutions, but the simple assurance that we are not alone.

Moral of the story:

"In the tapestry of life, love is not always woven with grand gestures and eloquent words. Sometimes, it is the silent threads of companionship, empathy, and unwavering support that create the most enduring patterns of healing and resilience."

XI
The Fall of a Titan

*"Pride is a gilded cage, its bars forged from our own
illusions of invincibility."*

The Titan's Ascent

In the heart of Mumbai, a city that pulsated with ambition and the relentless
pursuit of dreams, Rohan Mehra stood as a titan, his name synonymous
with power and success. The shimmering towers of Mehra Group of
Industries, a corporate empire that spanned continents, dominated the
skyline, a testament to Rohan's unwavering determination and his
extraordinary business acumen.

Born into a family of modest means, Rohan had clawed his way to the
top, his journey fueled by a burning desire to transcend his humble
beginnings and leave an indelible mark on the world. He was a self-made
billionaire, a charismatic leader whose vision and drive had transformed a
fledgling enterprise into a global powerhouse. His name was whispered in
awe in boardrooms and celebrated in the media, his every move scrutinized
and analyzed by those who sought to emulate his success.

The Intoxication of Power

But success, as it often does, came at a price. Rohan, once grounded and humble, found himself increasingly intoxicated by the allure of power and the intoxicating scent of wealth. He began to believe his own hype, his ego swelling with each acquisition, each successful deal, each glowing accolade. He saw himself as invincible, a master of his own destiny, immune to the vulnerabilities that plagued ordinary mortals.

He dismissed the cautious advice of his advisors, his arrogance blinding him to the potential pitfalls that lay ahead. "Trust me," he would declare, his voice filled with unshakeable confidence, "I know what I'm doing."

The Gathering Storm

Beneath the glittering facade of success, however, cracks began to appear. Rohan's relentless pursuit of expansion led him to make reckless decisions, his ambition outpacing his prudence. His foray into the international market was fueled more by ego than by sound strategy, his desire to conquer new territories overshadowing the need for careful planning and risk assessment.

His advisors, sensing the impending danger, grew increasingly anxious. But Rohan, his pride wounded by their lack of faith, brushed aside their concerns. "I don't need your doubts," he would retort, his voice laced with irritation. "I need your unwavering support."

The Perfect Storm

And then, the storm broke. A series of missteps, like a cascade of dominoes, began to unravel Rohan's meticulously crafted empire. A poorly managed acquisition in Europe resulted in massive layoffs and a barrage of lawsuits, tarnishing the Mehra Group's once-impeccable reputation. Social media erupted with calls for boycotts, and the company's stock price plummeted, wiping out billions of dollars in value.

As if that wasn't enough, a global recession struck, its icy grip tightening around the world's economies. Rohan's empire, built on a foundation of aggressive loans and overleveraged assets, began to crumble under the weight of its own ambition.

The final blow came when a trusted senior executive, a man Rohan had considered a close confidante, was exposed for embezzling millions of dollars, leaving the company's financials in a state of disarray. Rohan, who had prided himself on his ability to judge character and identify talent, realized with a sickening jolt that he had been blind to the betrayal brewing within his own inner circle.

The Fall

Within months, the Mehra Group of Industries, once a symbol of corporate dominance, was teetering on the brink of collapse. Rohan, the once-revered titan, found himself hounded by creditors, ridiculed by the media, and abandoned by the very people who had once sung his praises. The penthouse suite that had symbolized his success now felt like a gilded cage, its walls closing in on him, suffocating him with the weight of his failures.

The Reckoning

One evening, as the sun dipped below the horizon, casting long shadows across the Mumbai skyline, Rohan found himself alone in his opulent penthouse, the silence deafening, the emptiness overwhelming. He stared at the unopened letters piled high on his desk – legal notices, desperate pleas from employees who had lost their jobs, and angry demands from stockholders seeking accountability.

He remembered the words of Anil Deshpande, an old acquaintance who had cautioned him against the perils of pride. "Even Arjuna, the great warrior, couldn't escape fate," Anil had warned. "No wealth or power can shield us from what is written."

Rohan, his spirit broken and his ego shattered, finally understood the truth in Anil's words. He had believed himself to be invincible, a master of his own destiny. But in his relentless pursuit of power and wealth, he had lost sight of his own humanity, his own vulnerability.

The Return

The next morning, Rohan did something he hadn't done in years – he visited his mother. Sitting at the worn dining table in their modest family home, he poured out his heart, his voice trembling with regret and remorse. "Ma," he confessed, "I thought I was untouchable. I thought I could control everything."

His mother, her eyes filled with wisdom and compassion, smiled gently. "Rohan," she said, her voice soothing his troubled soul, "power and wealth are fleeting. What truly matters is how you face the storms. The world doesn't remember Arjuna for his defeats, but for his courage to rise again."

The Rise from Ashes

Inspired by his mother's words and the unwavering love of his family, Rohan embarked on a journey of redemption. He publicly apologized for his company's failures, acknowledging his own mistakes and taking responsibility for the consequences. He sold his penthouse, his luxury cars, and even some of his personal shares to repay his employees and creditors, his actions speaking louder than any words of remorse.

The media, initially skeptical, began to portray him in a new light – not as a fallen titan, but as a man determined to rebuild, to learn from his mistakes, and to emerge stronger from the ashes of his former empire.

Rohan started small, focusing on a single business unit, his approach now tempered with humility and a newfound appreciation for collaboration. He listened to his team, valuing their insights and expertise, his ego no longer clouding his judgment. Slowly but surely, he began to rebuild, not just his company, but his character, his integrity, and his reputation.

The True Measure of Success

Years later, at another gala dinner, a journalist approached Rohan, her microphone extended, her eyes filled with curiosity. "Mr. Mehra," she asked, "what would you say was your greatest success?"

Rohan smiled, his face etched with the wisdom gained through hardship and humility. "Understanding that power and wealth are temporary," he replied, his voice calm and steady. "True greatness lies in humility, resilience, and the ability to rise after a fall."

Moral of the story:

"No matter how high we climb on the ladder of success, pride and arrogance can lead to a devastating fall. True strength lies not in our

ability to control fate, but in our willingness to embrace humility, learn from our mistakes, and rise again with renewed purpose and integrity."

XII
The Inner Pilgrimage

"The longest journey is the one we take within ourselves, towards the temple of our own truth."

The Seeker's Restlessness

In the tranquil village of Jeevanapuram, nestled amidst the verdant foothills of the Eastern Ghats, where the air was filled with the fragrance of wildflowers and the gentle murmur of flowing streams, lived an old man named Parashuram. Revered by the villagers as a sage and philosopher, Parashuram possessed a wisdom that transcended the boundaries of books and scriptures. People from far and wide sought his counsel, their hearts burdened with questions, their minds yearning for answers. But Parashuram rarely spoke in sermons or grand pronouncements. He believed that life itself was the greatest teacher, its lessons etched into the fabric of experience, its wisdom revealed in the quiet moments of introspection and observation.

One sun-kissed morning, as the village awoke to the symphony of birdsong and the gentle rustling of leaves, a young man named Aravind arrived at Parashuram's doorstep. His eyes were filled with a restless yearning, his brow furrowed with the weight of unanswered questions. He had journeyed far and wide, his quest for truth leading him to temples and ashrams, to renowned scholars and spiritual masters. Yet, despite his tireless pursuit of knowledge, his heart remained unfulfilled, his spirit thirsting for a deeper understanding.

"Guruji," Aravind implored, bowing deeply before Parashuram, "I have wandered across sacred lands, read countless scriptures, and sought out the wisest of teachers. Yet, my heart remains restless, my mind a whirlwind of unanswered questions. Where can I find the ultimate truth?"

Parashuram smiled, his eyes twinkling with the serenity of one who had traversed the inner landscape and discovered the wellspring of wisdom within. "Aravind," he said, his voice gentle and reassuring, "you have searched far and wide, but you have overlooked the greatest temple, the purest river, and the wisest guru. Come, let us journey together, not to distant lands or sacred shrines, but to the inner sanctum of your own being."

The Journey Begins

Parashuram led Aravind to a small hill overlooking the village, where the morning sun painted the landscape in hues of gold and emerald. They sat beneath the shade of a majestic peepal tree, its leaves rustling like whispers of ancient wisdom. Parashuram began his teaching, his words as simple and profound as the truths they conveyed.

"Aravind," he said, "there is no temple greater than the body you inhabit. It is the most sacred dwelling place, the abode of your spirit, the instrument through which you experience the world. Just as you honor the sanctity of a temple, you must care for your body, nourish it, and respect its limitations. Neglect it, and your journey through life will falter. Strengthen it, and you will discover its divine potential."

Aravind listened intently as Parashuram placed his hand on his chest, his touch gentle but firm. "This body, Aravind," he continued, "is where your soul resides. Do not seek divinity outside yourself when you already carry it within. Your breath is the divine breath, your heartbeat the rhythm of the universe. Honor your body, and you honor the divine spark that dwells within you."

The River of the Mind

Their journey continued to a crystal-clear stream that meandered through the village, its waters reflecting the azure sky and the verdant landscape.

Parashuram knelt by the stream, his fingers gently caressing the flowing water.

"There is no river more sacred than your own mind, Aravind," he explained. "It is a sacred pilgrimage site, a source of endless possibilities. But remember, a river can either nourish or destroy, depending on how it is channeled. Let your mind flow towards truth, compassion, and wisdom, and it will cleanse your soul, carrying away the impurities of doubt and negativity. Allow it to wander aimlessly, to be swept away by the currents of fear and desire, and it will drown you in chaos and suffering."

Aravind knelt beside Parashuram, his gaze fixed on the flowing water, its surface mirroring the turbulence within his own mind. He had spent years searching for answers in the external world, in the noise and clamor of conflicting opinions and philosophies. He had neglected the inner landscape, the quiet sanctuary of his own thoughts and feelings. He vowed to cultivate his mind with the same care and attention that a gardener tends to a delicate flower, nurturing the seeds of wisdom and weeding out the weeds of negativity.

The Guru Within

As dusk painted the sky in hues of orange and purple, Parashuram led Aravind to a secluded cave, its entrance veiled by a curtain of vines. Inside, the silence was profound, broken only by the gentle dripping of water and the distant chirping of crickets.

"There is no guru greater than your own conscience, Aravind," Parashuram whispered, his voice echoing through the stillness of the cave. "The world will offer you countless guides, teachers, and philosophies, each claiming to hold the key to ultimate truth. But the true guru, the one who knows your heart and your path, resides within you. Listen to the whispers of your conscience, for it will never mislead you. It is the compass that points towards your true north, the inner voice that guides you towards your highest potential."

Tears welled up in Aravind's eyes as he realized the profound simplicity of Parashuram's words. He had spent his life searching for external validation, for a guru who could provide him with all the answers. But he had overlooked the most important guide of all – the one who resided within his own heart.

The Book of Life

As darkness enveloped the village, Parashuram and Aravind returned to the warmth of the fireside, the stars twinkling above them like celestial diamonds scattered across the velvet sky. Parashuram handed Aravind a blank book, its pages pristine and empty.

"There is no scripture greater than life itself, Aravind," he explained. "Every experience you endure, every encounter you have, every emotion you feel is a verse in the grand epic of your existence. The wisdom you seek is not written in ancient texts, but in the journey you undertake, in the lessons you learn, and in the transformations you undergo."

Aravind held the book tightly, its blank pages symbolizing the unwritten chapters of his life, the uncharted territories of experience that lay ahead. He realized that while he had sought knowledge in external sources, his true understanding would come from living life fully, from embracing its joys and sorrows, its triumphs and failures, with an open heart and a curious mind.

The Lesson of Experience

Finally, as the embers of the fire glowed softly in the darkness, Parashuram looked into Aravind's eyes, his gaze filled with wisdom and compassion. "There is no lesson greater than experience, Aravind," he said. "You can hear a thousand truths, read a hundred scriptures, and listen to countless sermons, but unless you live those truths, they will remain mere words, devoid of meaning and power."

Aravind understood. The answers he had been seeking were not to be found in distant lands or complex philosophies, but in the everyday moments of his life, in his interactions with others, in his struggles and triumphs, in his joys and sorrows. His journey wasn't about finding truth; it was about embodying it, about living a life aligned with his values, his conscience, and his deepest aspirations.

The Transformation

Years later, Aravind returned to Jeevanapuram, his spirit transformed by the inner pilgrimage he had undertaken. He had built a life of purpose and meaning, caring for his body, nurturing his mind, listening to the whispers of his conscience, and embracing the lessons of experience. People began to seek his guidance, drawn to the serenity that radiated from his being. And like Parashuram, he shared his wisdom not through grand pronouncements or complex teachings, but through simple stories and the quiet example of his own life.

One day, a young seeker, his eyes filled with the same restless yearning that had once consumed Aravind, approached him. "Guruji," he asked, "where can I find the ultimate truth?"

Aravind smiled, his face reflecting the wisdom he had gleaned from his inner journey. "My child," he replied, "there is no temple greater than your body, no river holier than your mind, no guru wiser than your soul, no scripture deeper than life itself, and no lesson more profound than experience. Begin your journey within, and you will find all that you seek."

Moral of the story:

"The greatest truths of life are not found in external sources, but within the depths of our own being. Honor your body, cultivate your mind, listen to your conscience, embrace life as your teacher, and embark on the inner pilgrimage that leads to self-discovery and the realization of your true potential."

XIII

The Cost of Ambition

"Ambition is a double-edged sword; it can carve a path to greatness, but it can also sever the ties that truly matter."

A Man who had everything, untill he had nothing

The Man Who Conquered the World

In the steel and glass canyons of Mumbai, where ambition roared like the Arabian Sea and dreams soared amidst the towering skyscrapers, Arvind Rao was a legend in the making. He was the CEO of AstraTech, a technology empire he had built with relentless determination, tireless effort, and an unwavering willingness to sacrifice everything in the pursuit of success. He was the epitome of the modern-day titan, the man who could turn failing businesses into profit-generating machines, the leader whose mere presence commanded respect and obedience in the cutthroat world of corporate warfare.

Arvind's days began before the sun peeked over the horizon, fueled by black coffee and an insatiable hunger for achievement. He would work late into the night, his mind a whirlwind of strategies, his phone a lifeline to a global network of contacts and collaborators. He scoffed at the notion of a 70-hour workweek, his ambition exceeding the boundaries of conventional time and commitment. "Seventy hours?" he would scoff, his voice laced with disdain. "Real leaders work 90! If you want to be the best, forget your weekends, forget your birthdays, forget your families. Success demands sacrifice."

And so, they sacrificed. His employees, inspired by his unwavering drive and seduced by the promise of wealth and recognition, pushed themselves to the limit, their lives revolving around deadlines, presentations, and the relentless pursuit of corporate goals. They sacrificed their personal lives, their relationships, and their own well-being on the altar of ambition, their sacrifices mirroring those of their revered leader.

The Family That Never Knew Him

Arvind's wife, Meera, once his confidante and lover, had become a stranger in their own home. She had spent countless evenings waiting for him at the dinner table, the food growing cold, the candles burning low. Eventually, she stopped setting his place, the empty chair a silent testament to his absence, both physical and emotional.

His daughter, Ananya, who had once clung to him with childish adoration, now spoke to him with the formality of a distant relative. Her laughter, which had once filled their home with joy, was now a rare and fleeting sound, a distant echo of a time when her father had been a constant presence in her life.

His son, Rohan, a budding athlete with dreams of glory on the football field, had long since stopped asking, "When will you come to my match, Papa?" He knew the answer, the unspoken truth that his father's ambition had eclipsed the simple joys of family and connection.

Arvind, however, remained oblivious to the growing chasm between himself and his loved ones. He was too consumed by the pursuit of wealth and power, his mind a prisoner of spreadsheets, projections, and the relentless demands of his corporate empire.

The Day the Sky Fell

It happened on a Wednesday, a day like any other in the high-stakes world of AstraTech. Arvind was in a crucial board meeting, his mind focused on the intricacies of a multi-billion dollar merger that would solidify his company's dominance in the global market. His phone vibrated, a persistent buzzing that disrupted the flow of his thoughts. It was Meera calling. He ignored it, his attention fixed on the task at hand.

Then came a text message, its words stark and chilling: "Arvind, Rohan met with an accident. He's in the ICU. Come soon."

The world seemed to tilt on its axis, the boardroom blurring around him. His heart pounded in his chest, a drumbeat of fear and dread. For the first time in his life, a business deal, a merger, a profit margin, seemed utterly insignificant.

He rushed out of the meeting, his colleagues staring after him in stunned silence. He raced through the city streets, his mind a whirlwind of guilt and terror. By the time he reached the hospital, it was too late.

His 14-year-old son, his beloved Rohan, was gone. A reckless driver, speeding through a crowded intersection, had struck him down as he cycled home from school. Rohan had called his father in his final moments, his voice weak and fading, but Arvind, consumed by his ambition, had not answered.

Meera, her eyes hollowed by grief, met Arvind's gaze, her voice devoid of tears but filled with a chilling accusation. "You were too busy," she said, her words piercing his heart like shards of glass. "Even Death couldn't wait for your schedule."

The Collapse

Rohan's funeral was a blur of white shrouds, weeping relatives, and murmured condolences. But the world, relentless and indifferent, did not stop for Arvind's grief. His office expected him back, his clients demanded his attention, his investors clamored for reassurance.

Arvind tried to immerse himself in work, to find solace in the familiar rhythms of spreadsheets and presentations. But something within him had shattered, a fundamental shift in his understanding of what truly mattered. The emptiness that had been gnawing at him for years now yawned like a chasm, threatening to swallow him whole.

One night, he sat at the dinner table in his sprawling, now-empty house. Meera had returned to her parents, taking Ananya with her. The silence was deafening, the loneliness unbearable. For the first time, Arvind truly saw the cost of his ambition. He had built an empire, but he had lost his kingdom, the kingdom of love, family, and connection.

The Final Lesson

The next morning, Arvind walked into his office, his footsteps echoing through the sterile corridors. He looked at his employees, their faces pale and drawn from long hours and relentless pressure, and a wave of realization washed over him. "What are we doing?" he asked, his voice filled with a newfound understanding. "We're killing ourselves for a company that won't shed a tear when we're gone."

And with that, he resigned. He walked away from the empire he had built, the wealth he had amassed, and the power he had wielded. He walked away from the gilded cage of ambition, seeking redemption in the ruins of his former life.

Months turned into a blur of introspection and regret. Arvind became a ghost of his former self, haunting the empty rooms of his house, staring at old photographs, replaying every missed opportunity, every neglected relationship, every sacrifice made in the name of ambition.

One evening, unable to bear the weight of his solitude any longer, he drove to his old house, hoping for a glimpse of Meera and Ananya. But the gate was locked, the windows dark. They had moved on, their lives no longer intertwined with his. He was alone, a stranger in the home he had once shared with his family.

That night, he checked into a hotel room, the city lights twinkling below like a cruel mockery of his shattered dreams. He sat by the window, a pen in his hand, and poured out his heart in a letter, a final testament to the lessons he had learned, the regrets he carried, and the wisdom he hoped to impart.

"To every man who thinks success is worth any price," he wrote, *"read this and think again. I had everything. A wife who loved me. Children who waited for me. Friends who missed me. I threw it all away for meetings, deadlines, and a corner office. But when I needed someone, I was alone. Don't let this be you."* — Arvind Rao

The next morning, they found him lifeless in his hotel room, a bottle of sleeping pills beside him, his letter a silent indictment of a life misspent.

The Message He Left Behind

At his funeral, his letter was read aloud, its words echoing through the somber gathering. It went viral, spreading like wildfire across the internet, its message resonating with millions who saw their own lives reflected in Arvind's tragic tale.

Some quit their jobs, seeking a better balance between work and family. Some went home early, eager to reconnect with loved ones they had neglected. Some called their parents after years of silence, their voices thick with emotion.

And for the first time in decades, corporate executives, their lives consumed by the relentless pursuit of profit and power, paused to reflect on the true meaning of success, the cost of ambition, and the enduring value of human connection.

Moral of the story:

"Success is meaningless if you have no one to share it with. The greatest regret of the dying is not the things they didn't achieve, but the moments they missed with those they loved. Don't be so busy making a living that you forget to live. Because in the end, your job will replace you within days, but your family will feel your absence forever."

XIV
The Price of Integrity

"Integrity is a flame that burns brightest in the face of corruption, but it can also consume the one who carries it."

A Lone Warrior's Fate

A Genius Forged in Simplicity

In the tranquil village of Thirunelli, nestled deep within the emerald embrace of Kerala's lush landscapes, a boy named Anirudh Swaminathan was born into a world of humble beginnings and soaring aspirations. His father, a dedicated schoolteacher with a passion for knowledge, instilled in him a love for learning, his mind a fertile ground where the seeds of curiosity blossomed into a thirst for understanding. His mother, a woman of quiet strength and unwavering compassion, nurtured his spirit, her gentle guidance shaping his heart and instilling in him a deep sense of empathy for his fellow human beings.

Anirudh was not merely intelligent; he was extraordinary. His mind, like a diamond, refracted knowledge, absorbing and synthesizing information with exceptional clarity and speed. He excelled in his studies, his academic achievements a testament to his intellectual prowess and his unwavering dedication to learning.

He topped the state in his 10th and 12th board exams, his scores setting a new benchmark for excellence. He secured the coveted All-India Rank 1 in the IIT entrance exam, his name echoing through the hallowed halls of IIT Madras, where he graduated with flying colors. And as if that wasn't enough, he cracked the IAS exam, once again securing the All-India Rank 1, his name becoming synonymous with academic brilliance and unwavering determination.

Universities across the globe, from the ivy-clad walls of Harvard and MIT to the historic colleges of Cambridge and Oxford, extended invitations, eager to welcome him into their prestigious programs. But Anirudh, his heart filled with a deep sense of patriotism and a burning desire to serve his nation, declined their offers. "I was educated with my country's money," he declared, his voice ringing with conviction. "It is my duty to serve its people."

The Unbending Will

And so, he embarked on a career as a civil servant, his idealism shining bright, his determination unwavering. He believed in the power of good governance, in the potential of the system to uplift the lives of the common man. He envisioned a society where justice, transparency, and efficiency prevailed, where corruption was eradicated, and where the voices of the marginalized were heard and respected.

His first few years in service were filled with hope and a sense of purpose. He took charge as a District Collector, his youthful energy and unwavering integrity a breath of fresh air in a system riddled with complacency and corruption. He tackled challenges head-on, his actions guided by his conscience and his unwavering commitment to serving the people.

When a private hospital, its greed outweighing its ethics, dumped toxic waste into the fertile farmlands, poisoning the soil and endangering the livelihoods of countless farmers, Anirudh shut it down without hesitation. The result? He was transferred the very next day, his superiors bowing to the pressure of powerful vested interests.

When a liquor mafia, its tentacles reaching deep into the corridors of power, evaded crores in taxes, Anirudh raided their warehouses, seizing their illicit goods and exposing their nefarious network. The result? A powerful minister, his pockets lined with the mafia's ill-gotten gains, threatened him, his voice laced with menace, warning him to back off.

And when Anirudh, his sense of justice unwavering, demolished an illegal construction that blocked public roads and endangered the lives of ordinary citizens, he discovered that the builder behind the project was none other than his own father-in-law. The result? His wife, torn between loyalty to her family and her husband's unwavering principles, left him, her parting words a bitter indictment of his unwavering commitment to duty. "You will always choose duty over family," she accused, her voice filled with pain and resentment.

The Price of Integrity

Yet, despite the setbacks, the betrayals, and the personal sacrifices, Anirudh did not break. His spirit, forged in the crucible of adversity, remained unyielding, his integrity a beacon of hope in a system shrouded in darkness.

He soon realized, however, that corruption was not just a disease; it was a deeply entrenched tradition, its roots intertwined with the very fabric of the system he had vowed to serve. In his new posting, he uncovered a massive scam, its tentacles reaching into the highest echelons of power. Government funds meant for building irrigation canals, funds intended to bring life-giving water to parched farmlands and alleviate the suffering of countless farmers, were being systematically looted by a network of corrupt contractors and officials.

Year after year, fake bills were created, projects were approved on paper but never implemented, and the same lake was "repaired" multiple times, its waters still overflowing during the monsoon season, flooding the fields and destroying the livelihoods of those it was meant to serve.

Anirudh, his conscience outraged by this blatant disregard for the welfare of the people, blocked all payments, demanding proof of actual work done. Within hours, his phone began to ring, the voices on the other end a chorus of threats and warnings.

"Approve the payments, and this can all go away," they hissed. "This is bigger than you. Don't make enemies you can't afford."

But Anirudh, his integrity unwavering, refused to yield. "The money belongs to the farmers," he declared, his voice ringing with defiance. "I will not let you steal it."

The next morning, he received his seventh transfer order in five years, his superiors hoping to silence him, to bury him in a bureaucratic backwater where his idealism would pose no threat to their corrupt schemes.

The Hero's Exile

The final blow came when the Chief Minister himself summoned Anirudh to his opulent office, the air thick with power and unspoken threats. "Anirudh," the Chief Minister said, his voice smooth but laced with steel, "you are an honest man, but the world doesn't work on honesty alone. We will put you in a post with no responsibilities. Consider it a paid holiday."

They didn't fire him. They didn't kill him. They simply erased him, consigning him to a bureaucratic purgatory where his talents and his integrity would be rendered irrelevant. No new projects, no staff, no work – just an empty office, a silent testament to the system's ability to neutralize those who dared to challenge its corrupt foundations.

But the world, it seemed, was watching. The United Nations, recognizing Anirudh's unwavering commitment to transparency and good governance, extended an invitation. They offered him a platform to share his expertise, to contribute to global initiatives aimed at combating corruption and promoting ethical leadership.

Anirudh, his heart heavy with disillusionment but his spirit still unbroken, made the hardest decision of his life. He walked away from the country he had loved and served, the country that had nurtured his dreams and then crushed his idealism. He walked away not because he wanted to, but because India, it seemed, did not deserve him.

Epilogue: A Nation's Loss

Today, Anirudh Swaminathan resides in Europe, his talents and expertise now benefiting the global community. He has authored 23 books on governance and ethics, his words inspiring a new generation of leaders committed to building a more just and equitable world. He has been awarded the prestigious Sahitya Akademi Award for his literary contributions, his voice reaching beyond borders and cultures.

He is respected worldwide, his name synonymous with integrity and courage. But in his own land, he is a forgotten hero, a casualty of a system that rewards conformity and punishes those who dare to challenge the status quo.

India did not fire him. India did not kill him. India simply made sure that he could never win. And that, my friends, is the greatest tragedy of all.

Moral of the story:

"Honest men are not always defeated; they are often erased, their voices silenced, their contributions marginalized. A nation that cannot protect its best and brightest will inevitably be ruled by the worst. History will remember those who fought for justice and integrity, even if they did not win. But the real question is, how many more Anirudhs must we lose before we realize the true cost of corruption and the urgent need for change?"

XV

The Unspoken Power

"In the realm of power, silence is not the absence of strength, but the wellspring of wisdom."

A Political Parable for Future Leaders

The Rise of Aditya Narayan Yadav

In the ancient city of Rajapura, nestled amidst rolling hills and the meandering currents of a mighty river, the legacy of intellectual giants and visionary leaders cast a long shadow. Over time, however, the political landscape had become a battleground of egos. The loudest voices often drowned out the whispers of wisdom, and the pursuit of power overshadowed the call to service.

Amidst this cacophony of ambition and deceit, a young leader named Aditya Narayan Yadav emerged. His presence was a quiet counterpoint to the prevailing chaos. He was not a scion of a political dynasty, nor did he possess vast wealth or influential connections. His strength lay in his wisdom, his patience, and his remarkable ability to harness the power of silence.

While his peers in the assembly engaged in heated debates, their voices echoing through the halls of power, Aditya listened intently. His mind absorbed the nuances of their arguments, and his intuition discerned the undercurrents of truth and deception. While others rushed to respond, eager to assert their dominance and defend their positions, Aditya paused. His silence was a strategic weapon that disarmed his opponents and earned him the respect of the people.

The First Test: The Power of Listening

One evening, a scandal erupted, its shockwaves rippling through the political landscape of Rajapura. Challa Raghunath Rao, a senior minister known for his integrity and dedication to public service, was accused of misusing public funds. The media, fueled by a thirst for sensationalism, demanded answers. Opposition leaders, sensing an opportunity to exploit the situation, launched scathing attacks on the government. And the public, their trust shaken, grew restless and disillusioned.

Aditya, as a rising star in the political arena, was expected to take a stand. Condemn the accused minister and appease the growing public outrage. His advisors, fearing a backlash that could damage his reputation and derail his political aspirations, urged him to speak out, to distance himself from the scandal, and reaffirm his commitment to transparency and accountability.

But Aditya, guided by his inner compass and his unwavering belief in the power of truth, remained silent. *"Be silent if you don't know the full story,"* He reminded himself, his voice a quiet echo in the midst of the storm.

Instead of joining the chorus of condemnation, Aditya embarked on a quiet investigation. His keen mind sifted through the evidence, and his intuition guided him toward the truth. And what he discovered shocked him to the core. Raghunath Rao was innocent, the victim of a carefully orchestrated plot by his rivals to destroy his reputation and seize his position.

Had Aditya succumbed to the pressure, had he spoken out prematurely, he would have unwittingly condemned an innocent man. He would have become a pawn in a game of political manipulation. But his silence, patience, and unwavering commitment to truth allowed him to uncover the deception and restore Raghunath Rao's honor.

When the truth finally emerged, the same media that had clamored for his condemnation now lauded his wisdom and restraint. The opposition leaders who had mocked his silence now feared his quiet strength and unwavering resolve. The people of Rajapura, too, learned a valuable lesson: *"A leader's power is not in how loud he speaks, but in how well he listens."*

The Second Test: Mastering Emotions

Politics, as Aditya soon learned, was not just a battleground of ideas and policies. It was also a crucible of emotions, where anger, resentment, and personal attacks were often used as weapons to undermine opponents and manipulate public opinion. His enemies, recognizing his composure as his greatest strength, sought to exploit his vulnerability. They wanted to provoke him into a display of anger that would tarnish his image and diminish his influence.

During a crucial budget discussion, a rival minister, his voice dripping with venom, launched a personal attack on Aditya's father, a respected teacher and pillar of the community. The assembly gasped, the air thick with tension. Aditya's supporters, their loyalty ignited by the insult, clenched their fists, ready to defend their leader's honor.

But Aditya, his mind trained in the art of emotional control, did not react. *"Be silent when you feel too emotional."* He reminded himself, his voice a calming presence in the midst of the storm.

Instead of retaliating, he smiled serenely and responded with quiet dignity. "We are here to discuss the people's future, not my past," he said, his words deflecting the attack and redirecting the focus to the issues at hand.

The rival minister, expecting an outburst, was left speechless. His attempt to provoke Aditya had backfired spectacularly. Aditya's composure, his unwavering focus on the greater good, won the day, his silence speaking volumes about his character and leadership.

The Third Test: Anger as a Weapon

Months later, Aditya faced his toughest challenge yet. The ruling party, threatened by his growing popularity and influence, concocted a plan to discredit him, to tarnish his reputation, and derail his political ascent. They fabricated a corruption case, the charges baseless but the potential damage immense.

The media, always eager for a scandal, seized upon the allegations, their headlines screaming accusations of wrongdoing and betrayal of public trust. Opposition leaders, sensing an opportunity to exploit the situation, joined the chorus of condemnation. Their voices were amplified by the echo chamber of social media. Even some within Aditya's own party, their loyalty wavering in the face of political expediency, began to distance themselves, their silence a tacit endorsement of the accusations.

Aditya's supporters, their faith in their leader unshaken, urged him to fight back, to launch a counteroffensive, to expose the lies, and defend his honor. But Aditya, his wisdom transcending the impulse for revenge, refused to be drawn into a battle fought on his opponents' terms. *"Be silent in the heat of anger,"* He counseled himself, his voice a steady anchor in the storm of accusations and innuendo.

Instead of engaging in a war of words, Aditya chose a different path. He ordered a transparent audit of all his government projects, opening every file to public scrutiny, inviting the world to examine his record and judge for themselves. He knew that truth, like a diamond, would ultimately shine through the mudslinging and deception.

Within weeks, the truth prevailed. The corruption charges crumbled under the weight of evidence, the real culprits exposed, their motives laid bare for all to see. The same people who had accused Aditya now found themselves apologizing, their reputations tarnished, their political ambitions thwarted.

Had Aditya reacted in anger, had he allowed his emotions to dictate his actions, he would have played into his enemies' hands. His defense would be perceived as weakness, his integrity questioned. But his silence, patience, and unwavering faith in justice had proven to be his greatest weapons.

The Ultimate Lesson: Silence that Builds Nations

As the years passed, Aditya Narayan Yadav rose through the ranks of the political landscape, his name becoming synonymous with wisdom, integrity, and effective leadership. But his greatest test came not from his political opponents, but from within his own party.

During a heated debate on agricultural reforms, Ramesh Pilot, Aditya's closest friend and political ally, expressed his opposition to Aditya's vision. The disagreement, fueled by differing ideologies and the pressures of political maneuvering, escalated into a public feud. Their once unbreakable bond was strained by the weight of conflicting opinions.

Ramesh, blinded by political ambition and the desire to assert his own influence, launched personal attacks against Aditya, his words echoing through the media, creating a rift within the party, and threatening to undermine their shared goals.

The media, eager to exploit the conflict, predicted a bitter showdown, a battle of egos that would weaken the party and jeopardize its hold on power. Aditya's followers, their loyalty fiercely protective, demanded retaliation, urging him to strike back at Ramesh and defend his honor.

But Aditya, his wisdom transcending the impulse for revenge, chose a different path. *"Be silent if your words can destroy a friendship,"* He reminded himself, his voice a quiet echo in the cacophony of demands and accusations.

He waited for the opportune moment, a moment when emotions had cooled, and reason could prevail. Then, he met Ramesh privately, their conversation a testament to the enduring power of friendship and the importance of placing principles above personal gain.

"If I must lose power to keep this friendship," Aditya confessed, his voice filled with sincerity, "I will."

His words, devoid of ego and filled with genuine concern for their relationship, melted Ramesh's anger and resentment. That very night, Ramesh withdrew his opposition to the agricultural reforms and issued a public apology. His actions were a testament to the transformative power of humility and forgiveness.

Their friendship, a cornerstone of their political alliance, was saved, and the nation's stability, threatened by their conflict, was restored.

Epilogue: The Leader Who Knew When to Speak and When to Be Silent

Aditya's journey through the treacherous landscape of politics was not one of grand speeches, fiery rhetoric, or self-aggrandizing pronouncements. It was a testament to the power of wisdom, restraint, and the strategic deployment of silence. His ability to hold his tongue when others lost theirs, to listen when others clamored to be heard, and to choose his words carefully, their impact amplified by their rarity, made him one of the most respected and effective leaders of his time. Long after he was gone, his legacy lived on, his name whispered in reverence by those who sought to emulate his leadership. Every young politician, eager to make their mark on the world, was taught the ultimate lesson: *"The strongest leaders are not those who speak the most, but those who know when to stay silent."*

Moral of the story:

"Words are powerful, but so is silence. Use both wisely, for they are the tools of a skilled communicator and a true leader.
A true leader listens more than he speaks, seeking to understand before seeking to be understood.
Emotional control is the greatest strength in the arena of politics, where passions run high and tempers often flare.
Never let anger dictate your actions, for it will cloud your judgment and lead you astray.
Silence, when used strategically, is the most potent weapon of all, capable of disarming opponents, revealing truths, and building bridges of understanding."

XVI
The Trail of Silence

"Silence is not always golden; sometimes, it is the weapon that inflicts the deepest wounds."

A Courtroom Drama on Emotional Abuse and Justice

Act I: The Gavel Falls

The grand courtroom of the Hyderabad High Court, its walls adorned with the scales of justice and the echoes of countless legal battles, was filled with an air of anticipation. The case of Meera vs. Arjun, a case that delved into the murky depths of emotional abuse and the invisible scars it inflicts, was about to be heard.

Meera, once a vibrant and hopeful woman, now stood before the court, her shoulders slumped under the weight of a marriage that had slowly eroded her spirit. Across from her sat Arjun, a successful corporate executive, his demeanor impassive, his eyes betraying no hint of the turmoil that lay beneath the surface.

"The court is now in session," announced Justice Karunakar Naidu, his voice resonating through the hushed chamber. "Advocate Sandeep Rao, you may present the case for the plaintiff."

Act II: The Case for the Plaintiff

Sandeep Rao, Meera's counsel, a man known for his sharp intellect and his unwavering commitment to justice, stepped forward, his presence commanding attention.

"My Lord," he began, his voice clear and resonant, "we are gathered here today not to discuss a crime of fists or weapons, but a crime of words and silence. Emotional abuse is the invisible wound, the silent killer that festers in the shadows, unpunished, unacknowledged. Today, we seek justice for my client, Meera, a woman whose spirit has been broken by years of systematic emotional abuse."

Meera, her gaze fixed on the floor, her hands trembling slightly, fought back tears as she listened to her lawyer's words. Years of ridicule, gaslighting, and relentless humiliation had stripped her of her confidence, leaving her feeling like a shadow of her former self.

Sandeep continued, his voice rising with righteous indignation. "Under Section 13(1)(ia) of the Hindu Marriage Act, 1955, my client seeks divorce on the grounds of mental cruelty. Under Section 3 of the Indian Evidence Act, we present medical records and psychiatric testimony to prove the psychological harm inflicted upon her by her husband."

A hush fell over the courtroom as Dr. Anita Varma, a renowned psychologist, was called to the stand.

"Dr. Varma," Sandeep inquired, "can you tell the court about Meera's condition?"

Dr. Varma, her voice calm and authoritative, cleared her throat. "Meera shows severe signs of emotional trauma, chronic anxiety, crippling self-doubt, and suicidal ideation. Years of psychological manipulation have led her to question her own worth, her own sanity."

The judge, his expression serious, nodded slowly, taking notes. Sandeep pressed on.

"And what, in your professional opinion, caused this trauma?"

Dr. Varma adjusted her glasses, her gaze steady and unwavering. "Constant belittling, gaslighting, and a complete disregard for her emotions. Arjun dismissed her dreams, humiliated her in front of friends and family, and controlled every aspect of her life, from her finances to her social interactions. This isn't just emotional neglect, My Lord; it is abuse, plain and simple."

A collective gasp rippled through the courtroom, the audience stunned by the stark reality of Meera's suffering.

"*Objection!*" *shouted Advocate Harish Menon, Arjun's defense counsel, his voice booming through the tense atmosphere. "This is nothing more than exaggeration! Marriage is built on adjustments, not accusations.*"

Act III: The Defense Strikes Back

Harish Menon, a seasoned lawyer known for his aggressive tactics and his ability to sway juries, stood up and strode towards the jury box, his confidence bordering on arrogance.

"My Lord," he declared, his voice dripping with sarcasm, "if we start criminalizing harsh words spoken in the heat of the moment, then every couple in the country would be behind bars! My client, Arjun, merely had high expectations for his wife. Is that a crime?"

He turned to Meera, his eyes narrowed, his voice laced with skepticism. "Mrs. Meera, are you claiming that harsh words are the equivalent of physical abuse?"

Meera, summoning her remaining strength, met his gaze, her voice surprisingly steady. "Yes, Advocate. A wound to the body heals with time. A wound to the soul lingers forever."

A wave of murmurs washed over the courtroom, the audience captivated by Meera's simple yet profound statement. Justice Naidu raised his hand, calling for silence.

"Continue, Advocate Menon," he instructed.

Harish smirked, his confidence unwavering. "Let us refer to Section 114 of the Indian Evidence Act," he countered. "Evidence must prove guilt beyond a reasonable doubt. Where is the proof that my client 'mentally tortured' his wife? Words can be misunderstood, twisted in hindsight to fit a particular narrative."

Sandeep Rao, unfazed by the defense's attempt to discredit Meera's testimony, stepped forward once more. "My Lord," he interjected, "let me remind this court of the Supreme Court ruling in Samar Ghosh v. Jaya Ghosh (2007), where the Honorable judges recognized that mental cruelty is as severe as physical cruelty in matrimonial cases."

He continued, his voice rising with conviction. "Furthermore, under Article 21 of the Constitution, every individual has the right to live with dignity. Meera was denied that right, her spirit crushed by years of systematic emotional abuse."

Justice Naidu nodded in acknowledgment, his expression thoughtful.

Sandeep turned towards Arjun, his eyes piercing through the facade of composure. "Mr. Arjun," he demanded, "tell me, when your wife cried herself to sleep every night, when she begged you to acknowledge her pain, when she tried to end her own life... did you ever ask why?"

Arjun opened his mouth to speak, but no words came out. His silence, a deafening echo in the tense courtroom, spoke volumes.

"Silence," Sandeep continued, his voice filled with quiet condemnation, "is the cruelest answer of all."

Act IV: The Verdict

The courtroom held its breath as Justice Naidu, his face etched with the weight of his decision, adjusted his glasses and prepared to deliver the verdict.

"The Constitution of India, under Article 21, guarantees the right to life and personal liberty, which includes the right to live with dignity," he declared, his voice resonating through the hushed chamber. "The Protection of Women from Domestic Violence Act, 2005, extends this protection to encompass psychological abuse, recognizing the devastating impact it can have on individuals and families."

He continued, his words carrying the weight of legal precedent and social responsibility. "Under Section 498A of the Indian Penal Code, cruelty, whether mental or physical, warrants legal action. Meera has provided substantial evidence of continuous psychological trauma inflicted upon her by her husband. The court recognizes emotional abuse as a legitimate ground for divorce under Section 13(1)(ia) of the Hindu Marriage Act."

A hush fell over the courtroom as Justice Naidu delivered the final judgment. "The marriage between Meera and Arjun is hereby dissolved. Furthermore, under Section 125 of the Criminal Procedure Code, the respondent is ordered to provide financial maintenance for his wife until she is self-sufficient."

A moment of stunned silence followed, broken only by the sharp rap of the gavel as Justice Naidu brought the proceedings to a close. The court had spoken.

Meera, her heart pounding with a mixture of relief and trepidation, exhaled slowly, the weight of years of silent suffering lifting from her shoulders. As she stepped out of the courtroom, the sunlight seemed to shine a little brighter, the world a little more hopeful. She was no longer just Meera, the victim; she was Meera, the survivor.

Final Reflection

The trial of Meera vs. Arjun set a legal precedent, a landmark judgment that recognized emotional abuse as a silent but devastating crime, one that leaves no visible bruises but can shatter a person's spirit and sense of self. Justice was served, not just for Meera, but for countless women suffering in silence, their voices muffled by fear, shame, and societal expectations.

For every unseen wound, there would now be a voice, a legal recourse, and a path towards healing and justice.

Moral of the story:

> "Emotional abuse is a crime, its wounds as real and as damaging as any physical injury. Silence is not always a virtue; sometimes, it is the weapon that inflicts the deepest pain. Speak up, seek help, and break the cycle of abuse. Justice, though sometimes delayed, will ultimately prevail."

XVII

The Unwavering Light

*"The flame of a lamp may flicker and fade, but the
light it casts can illuminate a lifetime."*

The Lamp-Maker's Wisdom

In a small town nestled amidst rolling hills and winding rivers, where the pace of life was as gentle as the rustling leaves and the warmth of human connection as comforting as the evening fire, lived a humble lamp-maker named Arunachalam. His craft, passed down through generations of skilled artisans, was more than just a trade; it was an art form, a way of weaving stories into the very fabric of light. Each lamp he crafted, its brass body gleaming with the patina of age and the touch of countless hands, carried within it the soul of a thousand tales, its glow a testament to the enduring power of human creativity and the timeless dance between darkness and light.

Arunachalam's shop, tucked away in a narrow alley of the town's bustling market, was a sanctuary of warmth and quiet contemplation. People came not just to purchase his exquisite lamps, but to bask in the gentle glow of his wisdom, his words as soothing as the soft flickering of candlelight.

Among those who frequented his shop was Vaidehi, a young schoolteacher whose eyes sparkled with intelligence and whose heart was filled with dreams as vast as the starlit sky. She admired Arunachalam's artistry, his patience, and his unwavering belief that every lamp he created had a destined owner, a soul whose path would be illuminated by its glow.

One evening, as the sun dipped below the horizon, painting the sky in hues of orange and purple, Vaidehi stood watching Arunachalam work, her curiosity piqued by his unwavering dedication to his craft.

"Master Arunachalam," she inquired, her voice filled with wonder, "don't you ever feel a tinge of sadness when you create something so beautiful, only to watch it leave your hands forever?"

The old man smiled, his wrinkled hands gently caressing the brass handle of a newly crafted lamp. "Vaidehi," he replied, his voice as warm and comforting as the flickering lamplight, "have you ever seen a flame try to hold onto its glow? No, because its purpose is to light the way, not to possess the light. And so it is with the lamps I create. Their purpose is not to adorn my shelves, but to illuminate the paths of others, to bring light into their homes and hearts."

Vaidehi pondered his words, her mind absorbing the deeper meaning behind his simple analogy. She understood that true artistry lay not in clinging to one's creations, but in releasing them into the world, allowing them to fulfill their purpose and bring joy to others.

The Journey Ahead

Months later, fate intervened, offering Vaidehi an opportunity that would change the course of her life. She received a prestigious teaching position in a distant city, a chance to pursue her dreams and make a difference on a larger scale. Yet, as the time to leave approached, she felt a pang of sadness, a reluctance to leave behind the familiar comforts of her small town and the people she had grown to love.

The night before her departure, she visited Arunachalam's shop one last time, her heart heavy with a mixture of excitement and trepidation. The old man, sensing her emotions, handed her a beautifully crafted lamp, its golden rim shimmering in the soft lamplight.

"Take this with you, Vaidehi," he said, his voice filled with warmth and encouragement. "It will remind you that what is meant to be yours will never be lost. Sometimes, we must journey far from home to fulfill our destiny, but the things that truly belong to us, the connections that truly matter, will always find their way back."

With a tearful farewell, Vaidehi left the familiar comforts of her small town and embarked on a new chapter in her life.

The Light Finds Its Way Back

Years passed, and Vaidehi flourished in her new environment. She excelled as a teacher, her passion for education igniting a spark in the hearts of countless students. She made new friends, built a new life, and embraced the challenges and opportunities that came her way. The wisdom of Arunachalam's words stayed with her, a guiding light in moments of uncertainty and doubt.

But time, as it often does, dimmed the memories of her past. The small town, the lamp-maker, and even the lamp he had gifted her faded into the background of her busy life.

Then, one day, a letter arrived, its edges worn, its ink faded. Arunachalam had passed away peacefully in his sleep, his spirit finally reunited with the eternal flame. His shop, now empty and silent, stood as a testament to a life well-lived, a life dedicated to creating beauty and sharing wisdom.

An Unbreakable Thread

Vaidehi, her heart filled with a mixture of sadness and gratitude, felt an irresistible pull drawing her back to the town where her journey had begun. She returned, her footsteps echoing through the familiar streets, the air filled with the same warmth and gentle rhythm, yet something was undeniably missing. The flickering lamps that had once adorned Arunachalam's shop were gone, their glow extinguished, their stories silenced.

As she entered the shop, dust motes danced in the fading light, the silence heavy with the weight of absence. But amidst the emptiness, she saw it – a single, untouched lamp, its brass body gleaming softly, its presence a beacon of hope in the gathering darkness.

As she reached for the lamp, her fingers brushed against a small piece of paper tucked beneath its base. It was a note, written in Arunachalam's familiar hand, its words a testament to his enduring wisdom and his unwavering belief in the interconnectedness of life.

"What is meant for you will always find its way back," the note read. "Some flames may flicker, some may fade, but the ones that belong to you will never be lost. You were never just a visitor, Vaidehi. You were the light that carried forward everything I ever believed in."

Tears welled up in Vaidehi's eyes as she realized the profound significance of the moment. The lamp she had once taken with her, the lamp that had symbolized her connection to Arunachalam and his wisdom, she had unknowingly left behind years ago. And yet, it had waited for her, its flame patiently biding its time, its glow a testament to the enduring power of their connection.

She lit the lamp, its golden light filling the empty shop, chasing away the shadows and illuminating the memories that had been tucked away in the corners of her heart. In that moment, she understood. What is truly yours, no matter the distance, no matter the time, will always find its way back home.

Moral of the story:

"What is meant for you will always find its way back. Love, opportunities, and even fleeting moments, if they are destined to be a part of your journey, will return, in one form or another. Hold things with open hands, not clenched fists, for true connections are never owned; they are merely experienced, cherished, and carried forward, their light illuminating our path long after they have seemingly faded away."

XVIII
The Revolt of the Unarmed

"When the oppressed find their voice, the walls of injustice crumble."

A Tale of Student Power and Social Justice

The Rise of Siddharth Yadav

In the heart of Uttar Pradesh, where the emerald tapestry of rice fields met the vibrant energy of college streets, stood the prestigious Prayagraj National University. It was a place where knowledge was meant to flourish, where young minds were nurtured, and where the leaders of tomorrow were forged. Yet, beneath the veneer of academic excellence, a darker reality festered. Power and privilege reigned supreme, creating a chasm between those born into wealth and influence and those who dared to dream beyond the confines of their humble beginnings.

The student union elections, a cornerstone of democratic participation, had become a twisted parody of their intended purpose. They were no longer a platform for the voices of the students, but a battleground where money, muscle, and political connections determined the outcome. The wealthy and well-connected manipulated the system, their influence casting a long shadow over the aspirations of those who lacked the resources to compete.

But the winds of change were stirring. Siddharth Yadav, a young man whose spirit burned with a fierce passion for justice and equality, stepped onto the stage, his presence a challenge to the established order.

Siddharth was not a child of privilege. The son of a retired schoolteacher and a farm laborer, he had witnessed firsthand the injustices that plagued his community, the deep-rooted inequalities that stifled the dreams of countless young people. His father, a man of quiet wisdom and unwavering principles, had instilled in him a profound belief in the power of education and the importance of fighting for a better world.

"If you want justice," his father had taught him, "*you must fight for it, not with weapons, but with wisdom.*"

Siddharth took those words to heart. He excelled in his studies, his mind a sponge for knowledge, his voice a beacon of reason in the often-heated debates that filled the university classrooms. He was passionate about law and social justice, his heart burning with a desire to create a more equitable society where everyone had the opportunity to thrive.

The Battle for Prayagraj University

In the student union elections, Siddharth decided to challenge the status quo. He announced his candidacy, his platform a call for transparency, accountability, and a student government that truly represented the voices of all students, not just the privileged few.

His opponent was Shiv Pratap Singh, the son of a powerful MLA, a young man whose arrogance and sense of entitlement were as boundless as his family's wealth and influence. Shiv Pratap didn't need to campaign; his father's money, his connections, and the implicit threat of violence were enough to ensure his victory.

The election campaign was a stark contrast in styles and resources. Siddharth, with his limited means and his unwavering belief in the power of truth, walked from hostel to hostel, from classroom to classroom, engaging in conversations with students, listening to their concerns, and sharing his vision for a more inclusive and just campus.

Shiv Pratap, on the other hand, relied on the tried and tested tactics of intimidation and manipulation. His posters plastered every wall, his rallies amplified by loudspeakers and the presence of hired muscle. His message was simple: *"If you have no power, you have no right to question the system."*

The System Fights Back

The system, as it often does, rallied to protect its own. Siddharth's posters were torn down overnight, his supporters threatened and intimidated. Teachers who dared to support him were pressured to remain neutral. And the university administration, under the influence of Shiv Pratap's powerful father, disqualified Siddharth's nomination on a flimsy technicality, their actions a blatant attempt to stifle dissent and maintain the status quo.

But Siddharth, his spirit undeterred, refused to be silenced. He understood that the power of the people, when united in a common cause, could overcome even the most formidable obstacles.

The Spark of Revolution

"If they hold the power," he declared, his voice ringing with conviction, "we hold the numbers."

He continued his campaign, his message resonating with students who had long felt marginalized and voiceless. He exposed the corruption that festered within the university, the unfair practices that favored the privileged few, and the fear-driven governance that stifled dissent and perpetuated inequality.

Within days, a student movement was born, its energy spreading like wildfire across the campus. Thousands of students, inspired by Siddharth's courage and his unwavering commitment to justice, rallied behind him, their voices rising in unison, demanding change.

Shiv Pratap and his father, initially amused by Siddharth's efforts, now watched with growing concern as the tide turned against them. "Students?" they scoffed. "What can students do? Rules exist for a reason. And rules are made by us!"

But Siddharth had already grasped a fundamental truth: Rules are chains for the weak and tools for the strong. But what happens when the weak refuse to wear their chains?

The Night of Justice

The day before the elections, the university administration, desperate to maintain control, declared the elections canceled, their decision a blatant disregard for the democratic process and the will of the students.

That was the final straw. That night, 15,000 students, their hearts filled with righteous anger and their voices united in a chorus of dissent, marched through the streets of Prayagraj. They carried torches, their flames illuminating the darkness, their chants echoing through the night. They surrounded the university, demanding a fair election, their presence a testament to the power of collective action.

Social media exploded with the hashtag #JusticeForPNU, the students' voices amplified by a global chorus of support. News channels covered the protest live, the images of students standing up for their rights beamed across the nation, capturing the attention of the public and putting pressure on the authorities.

The government, caught off guard by the scale and intensity of the student movement, was forced to back down. The High Court intervened, reinstating the elections and ordering the university administration to ensure a fair and transparent process. The police, who had been deployed to suppress the protests, were now instructed to protect the students and their right to peaceful assembly.

The Dawn of Justice

Election day arrived, and for the first time in years, the student union elections at Prayagraj National University were conducted without threats, bribes, or violence. The students, their voices finally heard, cast their votes, their ballots a testament to the power of unity and the unwavering pursuit of justice.

Siddharth won by an unprecedented margin, his victory a resounding mandate for change. As he stood before the cheering crowd, his election certificate held high, he addressed the students, his words echoing the spirit of their collective struggle. *"If you hold a gun, and I hold a gun, we talk about law,"* He declared, his voice ringing with conviction. *"If you hold a knife, and I hold a knife, we talk about rules. But when we stand together, unarmed and unafraid, we don't just talk, we change history!"*

The crowd erupted in cheers, their voices a symphony of hope and defiance, a testament to the transformative power of student activism and the unwavering pursuit of justice.

The Aftermath: A Lesson for Future Leaders

Shiv Pratap's father, humiliated by his son's defeat and the resounding victory of the student movement, vowed revenge. But the balance of power had shifted. The Chief Minister, recognizing the strength of the student movement and the public's growing support for Siddharth, ordered a reform of student elections across the state, ensuring transparency and fairness in all universities and colleges.

Shiv Pratap's father, once a symbol of unyielding power and influence, now found himself on the defensive, his authority diminished, his reputation tarnished. He had learned a valuable lesson, *"Power is not in money, power is not in weapons, power is in people who refuse to kneel."*

Siddharth's victory was more than just an election; it was a revolution, a testament to the power of collective action and the unwavering spirit of young people determined to create a better world. It was a lesson for future leaders, a reminder that true power lies not in wealth, privilege, or political connections, but in the hearts and minds of those who refuse to accept injustice and who dare to dream of a more equitable and just society.

Moral of the story:

"True power lies not in weapons, money, or politics, but in the collective strength of those who refuse to accept injustice.
Those who write the rules often break them first, but justice will always be rewritten by those who fight for it.
Laws, morality, and truth only hold value when they are based on equality and applied fairly to all.
A student movement is not just a protest; it is the first step towards a revolution, a powerful force for change that can challenge the status quo and create a better future."

৪০

XIX

The Man Who Became A Shadow

"The greatest tragedy is not death, but a life lived in the shadows, unseen, unheard, unloved."

The Slow Disappearance

In a quiet, middle-class neighborhood of Lucknow, where the rhythm of life was as predictable as the rising and setting of the sun, Anand Srivastava was once a pillar of stability, a man whose presence filled his home with a sense of warmth and security. For two decades, he had dedicated himself to his family, working tirelessly as a corporate manager, ensuring that his wife, Vasundhara, his 16-year-old daughter, Kavya, and his 14-year-old son, Rohan, never lacked for anything.

Anand was the quintessential provider, the man who never forgot a birthday, never missed a school event, and never allowed bills to pile up on the kitchen counter. He believed that love was best expressed through responsibility, through the unwavering fulfillment of his duties as a husband and a father. And for years, his presence in their lives was undeniable, his love a steady and reassuring force.

But when the company he had dedicated his life to unexpectedly shut down, leaving him jobless and adrift in a sea of uncertainty, everything changed. The foundations of his identity, the very pillars upon which he had built his sense of self-worth, crumbled beneath his feet.

The Shifting Sands of Support

At first, there was sympathy, a comforting chorus of well-wishes and reassurances.

"It happens, don't worry," his wife had consoled him, her voice filled with concern.

"You'll find something soon, Dad," his daughter had chimed in, her youthful optimism a temporary balm for his wounded pride.

But as the weeks turned into months, and the job offers failed to materialize, the sympathy dwindled, replaced by an uncomfortable silence. The questions about his job search became less frequent, the encouraging words less enthusiastic. And slowly, insidiously, the silence morphed into indifference.

The House That No Longer Saw Him

Anand, his confidence eroded by his unemployment and his sense of self-worth diminished by his inability to provide, began to doubt himself. "Maybe I'm overthinking," he would tell himself, his voice a whisper in the growing darkness. "Maybe it's just a phase. Maybe I'm being too sensitive."

But the subtle shifts in his family's behavior, the small acts of neglect, the unspoken dismissals, gradually formed a pattern that was impossible to ignore. No one asked about his job search anymore. No one invited him to join them for tea in the evenings. No one seemed to notice when he stopped shaving, stopped dressing up, stopped trying.

The final confirmation of his invisibility came one evening as he sat at the dinner table, a place where he had once presided over lively conversations and shared meals. "What's for dinner?" he asked, his voice tentative, his heart heavy with a sense of foreboding.

Kavya, her eyes glued to her phone, didn't even look up. "I ordered something for myself," she mumbled, her attention consumed by the digital world.

Rohan, his teenage son, barely acknowledged his father's presence. "I'm having a burger," he grunted, his focus fixed on the video game playing on his laptop.

Vasundhara, Anand's wife, was engrossed in a web series on her tablet, her laughter echoing through the room, a stark contrast to the silence that surrounded Anand.

No one had cooked at home. No one had thought of him. No one had even noticed his presence.

For the first time, a chilling question crept into Anand's mind: "What if I stopped eating? Would anyone notice?"

The Experiment

And so, he began an experiment, a desperate attempt to gauge his own significance in the lives of his family. He stopped eating at home.

Day 1: No one noticed.

Day 2: Still nothing.

Day 3: He ate at a local dhaba, the warmth of the food a poor substitute for the connection he craved.

At home, life went on as if he didn't exist. His family ate out, ordered in, or simply skipped meals altogether. Their world continued to revolve around their own individual pursuits, their own digital distractions, their own self-absorbed routines.

The Portrait in the Living Room

One evening, as the shadows lengthened and the house filled with a melancholic twilight, Anand stood in the living room, his gaze drawn to an old family portrait hanging on the wall. It was a picture taken years ago, a snapshot of a happier time when his children were young, his wife's smile radiant, and his own face filled with a sense of purpose and belonging.

He stared at his younger self, the man in the photograph, a man with dreams, ambitions, and a place in the world. "I used to be important," he thought, his heart aching with a longing for a time when he had felt valued, needed, seen. "When did I become... this?"

As he looked at his reflection in the glass covering the portrait, a harsh truth dawned on him. He had become like the portrait itself – always there, always visible, yet never truly seen. He was a fixture in their lives, a background presence, his worth measured solely by his ability to provide, his value diminished by his unemployment.

The Day He Left

One morning, Anand woke up and made a decision. He didn't argue, he didn't shout, he didn't leave a note. He simply walked out, his footsteps echoing through the silent house, his departure as unnoticed as his presence had become.

For the first time in years, he walked through the streets without a destination, his mind adrift in a sea of uncertainty and disillusionment. "How long will it take before they notice?" he wondered, a flicker of hope battling against the growing despair in his heart.

One day passed. Then two. A week. Still no phone calls, no frantic searches, no expressions of concern. And in that silence, in that stark absence of reaction, Anand finally understood. His absence meant nothing. He had become irrelevant, a ghost in his own home.

The Question That Changed Everything

Ten days later, driven by a desperate need for closure, Anand returned home. Not because they missed him, not because they needed him, but because he needed to know, to see for himself if anything had changed.

Nothing had.

His wife was still engrossed in her web series, her laughter echoing through the empty house. His daughter was still glued to her phone, her fingers flying across the screen, her world contained within the digital realm. His son was still playing video games, his headphones blocking out the world, his burger forgotten on the coffee table.

No one asked, "Where were you?"

No one cared.

Anand stood at the doorway, his heart heavy, his presence unnoticed. He waited, hoping against hope that someone would look up, would acknowledge his return, would express even a flicker of concern.

No one did.

That night, as he lay awake staring at the ceiling, a chilling question echoed through his mind: "Would it make a difference if I was gone?"

The Cold Truth

Days turned into weeks, and Anand continued his silent existence, a shadow moving through the motions of life, his presence a mere habit, his absence inconsequential.

One day, at a small café, a junior colleague from his old office greeted him warmly, his face breaking into a genuine smile.

"Sir," the young man said, his voice filled with admiration, "you always listened so patiently. It's rare to find someone who really hears you."

The words stung, their unexpected kindness a stark contrast to the indifference he encountered at home. Outside, in the world beyond his family, he was valued, respected, noticed. But at home, he was just a shadow, a silent presence that filled space but held no meaning.

The Final Realization

One evening, as he walked past the mirror in the hallway, Anand paused, his gaze drawn to the reflection staring back at him. He didn't recognize the man he saw. His eyes were dull, his shoulders slumped, his presence devoid of the vitality and purpose that had once defined him.

He took one last look at the portrait on the wall, the smiling man he used to be, the man who had once felt loved, needed, and valued.

"I don't belong here anymore," he whispered, his voice heavy with resignation.

And with that, he walked out the door, his footsteps echoing through the silent house, his departure this time final, irrevocable. He didn't wonder if they would notice, because now he knew they never would.

Moral of the story:

"A man is more than just a provider; he is a husband, a father, a friend, a human being with needs and desires for connection and love. Silence is the loudest scream of a neglected heart, a cry for attention that often goes unheard. Being surrounded by family doesn't mean you're not alone; sometimes, the deepest loneliness is felt in the midst of those we love the most.

No one should have to disappear to be noticed; love should be about presence, not just convenience.
A man's worth is not just in his paycheck, but in his presence, his love, and his contributions to the lives of those around him."

XX
Footprints in the Moon Light

"Though the body may be absent, the spirit lives on in the echoes of love and memory."

The Year of Silence

In the small village of Vrindavan, where the gentle rhythm of life was intertwined with the cycles of nature and the traditions of the land, Veer, a young boy of fourteen, found himself adrift in a sea of grief. His father, Somnath, a farmer whose wisdom was as deep as the roots of the ancient banyan tree and whose laughter was as warm as the summer sun, had passed away unexpectedly, leaving a void in Veer's life that seemed impossible to fill.

The world, once vibrant and full of promise, now felt muted and gray. Veer, his heart heavy with sorrow, retreated into a shell of silence, his laughter silenced, his once-boundless energy replaced by a quiet sadness that clung to him like a shadow.

His mother, her own grief a silent companion, watched with concern as her son withdrew from the world. She tried to offer comfort, but her words seemed to fall on deaf ears. Relatives and neighbors, their intentions kind but their words inadequate, offered empty platitudes.

"Be strong, Veer," they urged, their voices echoing the societal expectations that discouraged the open expression of grief.

"Your father would want you to take care of your mother," they reminded him, their words adding to the burden he already carried.

"Time heals everything," they assured him, their voices failing to soothe the raw ache in his heart.

But time, it seemed, was not healing anything. It only stretched the pain, making it more profound, more pervasive. The days turned into weeks, the weeks into months, and still, Veer's grief remained, a constant companion that cast a shadow over his every thought and action.

At night, when the village was enveloped in darkness and the stars twinkled like distant diamonds in the velvet sky, Veer would sit outside their small mud house, his gaze fixed on the heavens, his heart filled with unanswered questions.

"Where did you go, Paa?" he would whisper into the night, his voice barely audible above the chirping of crickets. "Why did you leave me so soon?"

The Dream That Changed Everything

One night, exactly a year after his father's passing, Veer had a dream, a vivid and surreal experience that would forever change his perspective on life, death, and the enduring power of love.

He found himself back in the familiar fields, the sun warm on his skin, the scent of freshly tilled soil filling his nostrils. He was sitting under their favorite banyan tree, its branches reaching towards the sky like welcoming arms. And across from him, his father sat, as real and as vibrant as he had ever been, his eyes twinkling with love, his smile as warm and comforting as the summer breeze.

"Why do you look so sad, Veer?" Somnath asked, his voice gentle and reassuring.

"Because you're gone, Paa," Veer whispered, his voice trembling with emotion.

His father chuckled softly, his eyes filled with a knowing light. "Gone? Who told you that?"

"I saw them burn you, Paa," Veer replied, his voice choked with tears. "I saw the pyre, the smoke, the ashes..."

Somnath shook his head, his expression filled with gentle amusement. "No, Veer. Look at yourself. Do you think I am truly gone? As long as you walk this earth, I live within you. Your hands, your voice, your strength – it is all me. And I am proud of you, my son."

Veer felt his throat tighten, tears welling up in his eyes. But his father just smiled, his presence a comforting beacon in the darkness of his grief.

"Whenever you miss me," Somnath continued, his voice a soothing whisper, "just walk barefoot on our land. I'll be there, in the soil, in the breeze, in your every breath."

And then, as the first rays of dawn painted the sky with hues of gold and rose, his father faded away, leaving Veer with a profound sense of peace and understanding.

The Awakening

Veer awoke with tears streaming down his face, but this time, they were not tears of sorrow or despair. They were tears of awakening, of a newfound connection to his father's spirit, a realization that death was not the end, but a transformation, a continuation of their bond in a different form.

He stepped outside, the world bathed in the soft glow of moonlight, the fields stretching before him like a silver tapestry, their silence a symphony of peace and tranquility. He took off his slippers and stepped onto the cool, moist soil, his bare feet sinking into the earth, his senses alive with the energy of the land.

And suddenly, he felt it – the warmth of his father's presence beneath his feet, the gentle caress of the wind on his face, the quiet wisdom of the land that Somnath had nurtured throughout his life.

"He was right," Veer murmured, his voice filled with wonder. "He never left."

As he walked through the moonlit fields that night, he did not walk alone. With every step, he felt his father beside him, his presence a comforting warmth, his spirit a guiding light.

The Eternal Bond

From that day forward, Veer's grief transformed into a source of strength and inspiration. He no longer mourned his father's absence, but celebrated his enduring presence in his life. He began to help his mother with the farm work, his hands calloused but his spirit filled with a newfound purpose. He excelled in his studies, his mind sharpened by a desire to honor his father's legacy. And every time he faced a challenge, every time he needed guidance, he would ask himself, "What would Papa do?"

The answers, he discovered, were not always clear or straightforward. But the process of asking the question, of seeking his father's wisdom within his own heart, brought him closer to Somnath's spirit, strengthening their bond and guiding him on his path.

He no longer waited for his father to return; he understood that Somnath had never truly left. All he had to do was look at his own hands, feel the breeze on his face, or walk barefoot on their land, and he would find his father there, always.

Moral of the story:

"Death is not the end; it is a transformation, a transition to a different realm of existence. Love and legacy continue beyond the physical limitations of life and death.
Our loved ones live on through us – in our actions, our memories, and the way we carry their teachings forward.
Sometimes, healing is not about moving on, but about realizing that those we have lost never truly left us. They are with us always, in the whispers of the wind, the warmth of the sun, and the depths of our own hearts."

XXI

The Unseen Goodbye

A Lesson in Lost Connections

"Success is nothing if it costs you the people who truly matter."

The Ascent: Chasing Success, Losing Sight

In the heart of Madurai, a city pulsating with the energy of devotion and ambition, Raghav stood tall, a symbol of entrepreneurial success. From humble beginnings, he had carved his path to prosperity, his journey a testament to his relentless drive, his sharp intellect, and his unwavering determination. He had transformed himself from a struggling student into a thriving entrepreneur, his name synonymous with innovation and achievement.

But Raghav's relentless pursuit of success had come at a cost. In his climb to the summit of achievement, he had slowly but surely detached himself from the people who had once formed the bedrock of his life, the friends who had cheered him on, supported him through his struggles, and celebrated his triumphs. Their calls went unanswered, their messages unread, their presence in his life fading like a distant echo.

Among those he had left behind was Vikram, his childhood companion, the friend who had shared his laughter and his tears, his dreams and his fears. Vikram, the one who had stitched together his torn school uniform, fought beside him in playground skirmishes, and listened patiently when the world seemed too loud and overwhelming.

Vikram had never sought recognition or reward for his friendship. He was the embodiment of selfless companionship, the kind of friend who gave without expectation, whose loyalty was as unwavering as the rising sun. But life, in its infinite wisdom, had a way of teaching its lessons through loss, through the painful realization of what we have taken for granted.

The Silence: When Absence Speaks Louder Than Words

"People rarely realize the value of those who love them unconditionally, until they are gone." One evening, as Raghav scrolled through the endless stream of messages on his phone, his mind numbed by the constant barrage of information, he stumbled upon an old text from Vikram. "Take care of yourself, my friend," the message read. *"Some things in life can't be rebuilt once broken."*

Raghav stared at the message, a wave of guilt washing over him. He had never replied. In fact, he could barely remember the last time he had spoken to Vikram. Weeks had turned into months, and somewhere along the way, Vikram had stopped trying. No angry messages, no confrontations, no accusations – just silence.

"Some people walk away quietly, not because they don't care, but because they're tired of proving that they do." Life, for Raghav, continued its relentless forward momentum. Deals were signed, accolades were received, and his business empire flourished. But amidst the trappings of success, a gnawing emptiness began to grow within him. He was surrounded by people who saw only his wealth, his power, his achievements. At home, conversations with his family were shallow and superficial. At work, friendships were transactional, based on mutual benefit and strategic alliances. He had everything he had ever dreamed of, yet something was undeniably missing.

The news of Vikram's departure from the city hit Raghav like a thunderbolt. No farewells, no explanations, no forwarding address – just gone. The realization that he had lost a friend, a true friend, whose value he had failed to recognize until it was too late, sent a shiver of regret through his soul.

The Realization: The Cost of Taking People for Granted

"When you finally realize someone's worth, you may only have their memories left." That night, as Raghav lay awake in his luxurious bed, the city lights painting patterns on his ceiling, a question haunted his thoughts: Would it make a difference if he was gone? Would anyone truly miss him? Or was he just a name on their contact lists, a stepping stone in their careers, a provider of resources?

The more he pondered, the clearer the answer became. Vikram had been irreplaceable, his presence a quiet but constant source of support, his loyalty unwavering, his friendship a treasure he had taken for granted. Vikram had never asked for anything in return, except his time, his attention, his acknowledgment. And even that, Raghav had failed to give.

"You will never regret prioritizing the right people. But you will regret realizing their worth too late." Raghav searched for Vikram in others, hoping to find that same warmth, that same quiet loyalty, that same unwavering support. But he never did. Because some people are once-in-a-lifetime treasures, and once lost, they can never be replaced.

The Redemption: What Truly Matters in the End

"Your greatest investment is in the people who love you when you have nothing to offer." Determined to make amends, to salvage what he could of their friendship, Raghav traveled to Vikram's new home, a small, peaceful village where the air was clean, the pace of life was slower, and the people spoke in smiles rather than transactions. He found Vikram teaching at a local school, his passion for education undimmed, his spirit still shining bright.

As Raghav approached, Vikram greeted him warmly, but there was a distance in his eyes, a polite familiarity that replaced the deep connection they had once shared. It was a goodbye that had never been spoken, a loss that had been accepted.

"I'm sorry, Vikram," Raghav said, his voice filled with regret. "I never meant to... forget."

Vikram smiled, but his eyes held a knowing sadness. "Life is funny, isn't it?" he replied. "We chase things we think will last forever and forget the ones who were there from the start. But don't worry, Raghav. I understand."

Raghav realized then that it wasn't about grand apologies or dramatic reunions. Some things, once lost, cannot be fully recovered. The threads of their friendship, once woven so tightly, had been frayed by neglect, and though they might still be connected, the fabric would never be the same.

"Some friendships are like glass – once shattered, even the best glue can't make them whole again." He had come searching for his old friend, but what he found was a stranger with a familiar face, a man who had moved on, who had accepted the loss of their connection. It was a lesson learned too late, a price paid for taking a precious gift for granted.

Moral of the story:

"Never let success blind you to the people who truly care for you, those whose love is not contingent on your achievements or your possessions.
Some people walk away not because they stopped caring, but because they got tired of proving their worth.
The people who see you beyond your achievements, who love you for who you are, not what you have, are the ones who truly matter.
Cherish them before they become memories."

Final Thought:

"We don't lose people by chance. We lose them by choice – the choices we make every day when we fail to prioritize them. Some goodbyes don't come with a warning; they just happen. Don't let the people who truly matter slip away unnoticed."

৪৩

XXII

The Rangoli of Self

"The greatest journey is the one we take to rediscover ourselves."

A Faded Melody

In the vibrant city of Madurai, where ancient temples stood as silent witnesses to the ebb and flow of human emotions, Anika's love for Rohan burned like an eternal flame, its warmth enveloping him, its light guiding his path. Her world revolved around him, her every thought and action dedicated to his well-being, his ambitions, and the needs of his family. Anika, once a spirited Kathak dancer whose anklets jingled with joyous abandon, found her own rhythm fading, her movements hesitant, her spirit dimmed by the subtle expectations and unspoken demands of her traditional in-laws.

"The soul is placed in the body like a precious jewel, and its light must not be dimmed."

Rohan's family, steeped in the customs and traditions of their ancestors, held a vision of the ideal wife and daughter-in-law – a woman who devoted herself entirely to her husband and his family, her own aspirations subservient to the needs of the household. Anika, eager to please and to secure her place within the family, embraced this role with unwavering fervor. She became the supportive partner, the dutiful daughter-in-law, her own dreams and desires relegated to the shadows.

Her ghungroos, once an extension of her vibrant spirit, gathered dust in a forgotten corner of their home, their silent protest a poignant reminder of the dancer she had once been, the artist whose soul yearned to express itself through the graceful movements and rhythmic footwork of Kathak.

The Erosion of Identity

Years flowed by like the sacred Ganges, carrying with them the remnants of Anika's forgotten dreams. Her laughter, once a melodious raga that filled their home with joy, became a soft accompaniment to Rohan's triumphs, her own happiness contingent on his success. The colorful sarees she had once adorned, a reflection of her artistic spirit and her zest for life, were replaced by muted hues, their vibrancy dimmed, their patterns mirroring the subtle erosion of her own identity.

She was no longer Anika, the dancer, the artist whose movements spoke a language that transcended words. She was Anika, Rohan's wife, and later, Anika, Rohan's mother, her roles defined by her relationship to others, her own individuality fading into the background.

While Rohan's career soared like a kite in the boundless sky, his architectural designs earning him accolades and recognition, Anika's spirit dimmed, like a diya struggling to stay alight in the face of a relentless wind. *"The greatest loss is not of material things, but of the self."*

The Unspoken Acknowledgment

During Diwali, the festival of lights, Rohan received a prestigious award for his architectural contributions to the city. His acceptance speech was a heartfelt expression of gratitude, his words acknowledging the support of his family, his mentors, and his colleagues. Yet, Anika's name remained unspoken, not out of malice or ingratitude, but out of an ingrained habit of overlooking her contributions, her sacrifices, and her very existence as an individual.

Rohan, blinded by his own success and the societal expectations that shaped his perception, simply didn't see her, not the real Anika, the woman who had given up her dreams to support his, the woman whose spirit had been slowly extinguished in the shadows of his ambition. *"We see the world not as it is, but as we are."*

The Reflection in the Shadows

That night, as the Diwali lights twinkled like a million stars, casting long shadows across their home, Anika stood before the mirror, her gaze fixed on the reflection staring back at her. The woman she saw was a stranger, her eyes tired, her smile hesitant, her spirit shrouded in a veil of sadness.

Where was the dancer, the artist who had once painted vibrant rangolis on their doorstep, her fingers dancing across the floor, creating patterns of color and joy? Where was the laughter that had once filled their home, the carefree spirit that had once danced to the rhythm of her own heart?

The realization struck her like a summer storm, its intensity shaking her to the core. She had lost herself in the act of loving, giving so much of herself to others that she had nothing left for herself. *"Know thyself, for within you lies the universe."*

A Spark of Resilience

The pain of this realization was searing, like a chili pepper igniting her senses. But within that pain, a spark of resilience ignited, a refusal to fade away, to become a ghost in her own life. She would not disappear, she would not be silenced, she would not allow her spirit to be extinguished. She would reclaim her identity, her "atma," the essence of who she was and who she was meant to be. *"Arise, awake, and stop not till the goal is reached."*

The Journey of Rediscovery

Anika's journey back to herself was not a sudden transformation, a dramatic Bollywood-style makeover. It was a slow, deliberate process, like a lotus flower unfolding its petals in the morning sun.

She dusted off her ghungroos, their tarnished brass gleaming with the promise of renewed purpose. She started small, a few hesitant steps in the privacy of her room, her body remembering the forgotten language of rhythm and grace. Gradually, her confidence grew, her movements regaining their fluidity, her spirit reawakening with each twirl and stomp of her feet.

She reconnected with her guru, the teacher who had nurtured her passion for dance, her heart filled with gratitude for the wisdom and guidance that had once ignited her soul. She practiced diligently, her body and mind rediscovering the joy of movement, the power of expression, the freedom of self-discovery.

And she began to say "no," a small but powerful word that marked the boundaries of her newfound self-respect. She gently but firmly asserted her needs, her desires, her right to pursue her own dreams and passions. *"The journey of a thousand miles begins with a single step."*

The Difficult Conversation

Rohan, initially taken aback by Anika's transformation, resisted her attempts to reclaim her space, her identity, her voice. He had grown accustomed to her quiet acquiescence, her unwavering support, her willingness to sacrifice her own aspirations for his. But Anika, her spirit now anchored in a newfound sense of self-worth, would not be swayed.

She explained, not with anger or resentment, but with quiet determination, that loving him did not mean sacrificing her own identity, her own dreams. It was a difficult conversation, filled with tears, unspoken resentments, and the weight of years of unspoken expectations. But it was a necessary conversation, a cleansing process that allowed them to confront the imbalances in their relationship and forge a new path forward, one based on mutual respect, understanding, and the recognition of each other's individuality. *"Speak the truth, even if it is bitter."*

Emerging from the Shadows

Slowly, painstakingly, Anika emerged from the shadows, her spirit rekindled, her light shining brighter than ever before. Her laughter returned, richer and more genuine than before, like the melodious chimes of temple bells. Her sarees regained their vibrant hues, their patterns a celebration of her reawakened spirit. And her dance, once a forgotten language, became her voice, her expression, her truth.

She began teaching Kathak to young girls, her passion for dance now a legacy passed on to a new generation, her movements a testament to the enduring power of art to heal, to inspire, and to connect us to our deepest selves. *"The purpose of life is to find your gift. The work of life is to develop it. The meaning of life is to give it away."*

The Complete Woman

Anika's journey was not about abandoning love or rejecting her role as a wife and mother. It was about understanding that true love begins with loving oneself, with honoring one's own spirit, with recognizing one's own inherent worth. It was about realizing that her light was just as important as anyone else's, that her dreams and aspirations deserved to be nurtured and celebrated. And it was about finally seeing herself in the mirror, not as a shadow or a reflection of someone else's expectations, but as a vibrant, complete woman, a masterpiece in progress. "The sun shines not for the asking, but because it has light within."

Moral of the story:

"*Never lose yourself in the act of loving. Your identity, your dreams, your spirit – these are precious and must be cherished. True love begins with self-love, with the recognition that your light is just as important as anyone else's. Embrace your passions, pursue your dreams, and never allow your spirit to be dimmed by the expectations of others.*"

XXIII

The Whispers of the Unseen Summit

*"The mountain whispers its secrets to those who dare
to listen."*

The Uncomfortable Ascent

Anya's breath mingled with the biting wind as she clung to the sheer face of Mount Kailash, her fingers raw, her muscles screaming in protest. The majestic peak, shrouded in mist and mystery, loomed above her, its summit a distant beacon in the vast expanse of the Himalayas. Doubt, a relentless companion on this arduous journey, whispered insidious suggestions of retreat, its voice amplified by the thin air and the unforgiving terrain. *"The mountain tests not your strength, but your resolve."*

This climb, Anya knew, was not just about conquering a physical challenge; it was about conquering the doubts and fears that had held her captive for far too long. It was about proving to herself, and to the world, that she was capable of pushing beyond her perceived limitations, of achieving the extraordinary.

She remembered her grandfather's words, spoken with the wisdom of a life lived in harmony with nature's challenges: *"Discomfort is the forge where resilience is tempered."*

Each painful step, each labored breath, each moment of doubt and uncertainty was a testament to her refusal to surrender. She would not allow the whispers of fear to drown out the voice of her own determination. She would not let the discomfort of the climb deter her from reaching the summit, the summit that represented not just a physical destination, but a personal triumph.

The Slow Burn of Progress

Days blurred into a relentless cycle of climbing, resting, and climbing again. Progress was agonizingly slow, each upward inch gained at the cost of immense effort, each milestone a testament to her unwavering perseverance. There were moments when the sheer scale of the mountain seemed to mock her, its imposing presence dwarfing her struggles, its silence a deafening reminder of her own insignificance in the face of nature's grandeur. *"True progress is measured not in miles, but in the transformation of the climber."*

Anya wasn't climbing for applause or recognition. She wasn't seeking the fleeting satisfaction of external validation. She was climbing for herself, for the woman she aspired to become, the woman who refused to be defined by her fears or her limitations.

The Unseen Audience

Anya knew that few understood her obsession with Mount Kailash. They saw it as a pointless, even reckless pursuit, a waste of time and energy. Their lack of understanding, however, did not sting as much as the quiet voice within her that sometimes questioned her own sanity. *"The vision that drives you is yours alone to see."*

She wasn't seeking their approval or their admiration. Her motivation came from a deeper place, a promise she had made to herself years ago, a vow to push her limits, to test her boundaries, and to discover the strength that lay dormant within her. *"Self-belief is the compass that guides you through the fog of doubt."*

The Promise to Self

Quitting was tempting, a siren song promising relief from the pain, the exhaustion, the uncertainty. But Anya knew that surrendering would be a betrayal, a broken promise to the girl who had dreamed of reaching the summit, the girl who had refused to be defined by her limitations. *"A promise to oneself is the most sacred of vows."*

She thought of her late grandmother, a woman of quiet strength and unwavering determination, who had always encouraged her to pursue her dreams, no matter how audacious or unconventional. *"The only limits that truly bind you are the ones you set yourself,"* her grandmother had often said, her words a guiding light in Anya's darkest moments.

The Redefined Possible

Anya wasn't here to settle for a life of comfort and mediocrity. She was here to redefine what was possible, not just for herself, but for anyone who had ever dared to dream beyond the confines of their present circumstances. *"Mediocrity is a cage built by those who fear their own potential."*

She was driven by an inner fire, a relentless desire to push past the boundaries of her perceived limitations, to explore the uncharted territories of her own capabilities. *"The uncommon path is rarely paved with applause, but it leads to extraordinary destinations."*

The Uncommon Ascent

And so, she climbed, her spirit soaring with each upward step, her determination fueled by the whispers of the mountain, the whispers that spoke of resilience, perseverance, and the boundless potential of the human spirit.

Finally, after days of relentless effort, Anya reached the summit. There were no fireworks, no fanfare, no cheering crowds. Just the quiet majesty of the surrounding peaks, their snow-capped summits piercing the azure sky, and the profound sense of accomplishment that washed over her, filling her with a sense of peace and fulfillment that transcended any external reward.

The view was breathtaking, a panoramic vista of snow-covered mountains, verdant valleys, and winding rivers. But the true transformation had happened within. Anya had faced her fears, conquered her doubts, and emerged stronger, more resilient, more herself. *"The true summit lies not at the top of the mountain, but within the climber."*

Anya had become uncommon, not because of her achievement, but because of her unwavering commitment to her own potential, her refusal to be defined by the limitations others had placed upon her. *"Uncommon is not a destination, it's a way of being."*

Moral of the story:

"The uncommon path is rarely paved with applause, but it leads to extraordinary destinations.
Believe in your vision, keep your promises to yourself, and redefine what's possible.
The true summit lies not at the top of the mountain, but within the climber."

XXIV

A Song of Two Souls

"When two souls resonate in harmony, their love becomes a symphony that echoes through eternity."

The Legend of Indrani and Madhava

The Search for Resonance

In the ancient city of Avanti, where the sacred Shipra River flowed like a melody through the heart of the land, Indrani, a gifted musician, poured her soul into her art. Her voice, as enchanting as the songs of celestial apsaras, had the power to soothe troubled hearts, ignite passions, and transport listeners to realms of ethereal beauty. Yet, despite the admiration she received, Indrani felt a profound emptiness, a yearning for a connection that transcended the superficial praise and fleeting applause. *"The notes I play are but echoes until they find a heart that understands their silent song."*

Across the winding lanes of Avanti, amidst the bustling markets and the serene temples, lived Madhava, a visionary artist whose canvases pulsed with the vibrant energy of life itself. His colors danced with the rhythm of the cosmos, his brushstrokes capturing the ephemeral beauty of the human spirit, his art a reflection of the divine spark that resided within all beings.

Yet, Madhava, too, felt a void, a longing for a kindred spirit, a muse who could ignite the fire of his creativity and comprehend the depths of his artistic vision. *"Art is the language of the soul, but it needs a kindred spirit to truly decipher its meaning."*

Destiny's Whisper

Fate, in its mysterious ways, orchestrated their encounter during the annual spring festival, a celebration of love, renewal, and the blossoming of new beginnings. Indrani's music filled the air, its melodies weaving a tapestry of enchantment that captivated the hearts of all who listened. Madhava's paintings adorned the festival grounds, their vibrant colors and evocative forms capturing the spirit of joyous abandon and the celebration of life.

Their eyes met across the crowded marketplace, a spark igniting between two souls destined to intertwine, their paths converging in a symphony of shared passions and unspoken desires. *"Destiny whispers in the glances of those meant to meet."*

Drawn together by an invisible force, Indrani and Madhava embarked on a journey of shared discovery, their hearts resonating with a harmony that transcended the boundaries of their individual art forms. They explored the ancient scriptures together, delving into the profound wisdom of the Vedas and the Upanishads, their conversations weaving a tapestry of philosophical insights and spiritual revelations.

They discussed the concept of 'Prema Bhakti', the path of divine love, where devotion and surrender become the pathways to liberation. They explored the 'Rasas', the aesthetic flavors of human experience, recognizing the power of art to evoke a spectrum of emotions, from the joyous and uplifting to the melancholic and introspective. And they pondered the nature of the 'Atman', the individual soul, and its connection to 'Brahman', the ultimate reality, the source of all creation. *"Love is not merely a feeling; it is the thread that connects the Atman to Brahman."*

The Alchemy of Love

Inspired by their shared understanding and their deepening connection, Indrani's music underwent a profound transformation. Her melodies, once a reflection of her own individual experiences and emotions, now resonated with the wisdom of the ages, the cosmic dance of creation, and the boundless love that permeated the universe.

"My music was a search," she confessed to Madhava, her voice filled with gratitude, "but now it is a finding – a finding of you, and of the love that binds us."

Madhava's art, too, underwent a metamorphosis, mirroring the blossoming of their love and the deepening of their spiritual connection. His colors radiated with the light of enlightenment, his forms embodying the essence of pure emotion, his brushstrokes capturing the interconnectedness of all beings.

"My art was a mirror, reflecting the world," he mused, his eyes sparkling with newfound clarity. "Now, it is a window, revealing the depths of the heart."

A Symphony of Souls

On the auspicious day of Vasant Panchami, the festival of spring and love, Indrani and Madhava unveiled their artistic creations to the world, their offerings a testament to the transformative power of love and the profound connection between art and spirituality.

Indrani's concert was a spiritual awakening, her voice soaring through the ancient halls of Avanti, her melodies transporting the audience to a realm of pure bliss and transcendental beauty.

"Let the music wash away your worries and fill your soul with the nectar of love," she urged, her voice a conduit for the divine energy that flowed through her.

Madhava's exhibition was a visual feast, his paintings a symphony of colors and forms that spoke a universal language, revealing the interconnectedness of all beings and the inherent beauty that resided within each soul.

"Each brushstroke is a prayer," he explained, his voice filled with reverence, "each color a song of unity."

Their art, born from the crucible of their love and their shared spiritual journey, became a beacon of inspiration for the people of Avanti. It reminded them that love, in its purest form, is not merely a romantic sentiment, but a transformative force that can elevate the human spirit, heal the wounds of the past, and unite individual souls with the divine.

Indrani and Madhava's Vasant Panchami celebration was not just a romantic union; it was a philosophical declaration, a testament to the power of love to transcend the mundane and lead us towards self-realization and liberation. "*Love is the journey, the destination, and the map that guides us home.*"

Moral of the story:

"True love is not just a romantic connection; it is a spiritual union that can inspire, transform, and elevate the human spirit. When two souls resonate in harmony, their love becomes a symphony that echoes through eternity, its melody a testament to the interconnectedness of all beings and the boundless potential of the human heart."

XXV

The Jasmine's Unfolding

"The heart's melody should not be silenced by the world's expectations."

The Whispers of the Village

In the small village of Thiruvaiyaru, nestled amidst the lush green fields and ancient temples of Tamil Nadu, Mythili's spirit bloomed like a lotus flower, its petals unfurling in defiance of the stifling expectations that surrounded her. From the time she was a young girl, the whispers of tradition had dictated the course of her life, their voices echoing the age-old customs and societal norms that defined the roles of women in their community.

"Excel in your studies," they urged, their words shaping her path towards academic achievement.

"Marry a suitable groom chosen by your family," they instructed, their voices reinforcing the patriarchal structures that governed their lives.

"Dedicate your life to domesticity," they commanded, their expectations stifling her dreams and aspirations.

But Mythili, her heart filled with a passion that defied convention, harbored a different vision for her future. She yearned to become a Carnatic music vocalist, her voice soaring through the hallowed halls of ancient temples, her melodies echoing the divine ragas that had been passed down through generations of musicians.

The Courage to Deviate

Mythili's passion for music was met with raised eyebrows and hushed disapproval. "Music is a hobby, not a career," the villagers whispered, their voices laced with judgment and concern. "A woman's place is in the home, not on the stage."

But Mythili's spirit, as vibrant and resilient as the hues of her Kanjeevaram sarees, refused to be dimmed. She knew that her path was different, that it diverged from the well-trodden road laid out for her by tradition and societal expectations. *"The truest path is the one you carve for yourself."*

She practiced in secret, her voice weaving through the quiet hours of the night, a symphony of rebellion against the constraints that sought to confine her. Her melodies, filled with longing and determination, echoed through the moonlit fields, a testament to her unwavering spirit and her refusal to be silenced.

The Unwavering Voice

Mythili's family, steeped in the traditions of their ancestors, struggled to comprehend her aspirations. Her mother, though loving and supportive, pleaded with her to conform, fearing the judgment of their community and the potential consequences of defying societal norms. Her father, a respected village elder, remained silent, his disappointment a heavy presence in their home, a constant reminder of the chasm that separated their dreams for her future. *"The courage to be oneself is the highest form of devotion."*

But Mythili, her heart filled with a conviction that transcended the fear of disapproval, refused to abandon her dreams. She auditioned for a prestigious music school in Chennai, her voice trembling with a mixture of excitement and trepidation. Rejection followed rejection, each setback a test of her resilience, a challenge to her self-belief. *"Rejection is not a full stop, but a comma in the story of your dreams."*

Undeterred, she continued to hone her skills, practicing tirelessly, pouring her soul into every note, her voice growing stronger, richer, more expressive with each passing day.

The Test of Love

As Mythili's musical journey unfolded, her family, concerned about her future and their own reputation in the village, arranged a marriage proposal. The groom, a successful engineer from a well-respected family, represented everything they deemed desirable in a son-in-law. But he also expected Mythili to conform to the traditional role of a wife, to abandon her musical aspirations and dedicate herself to domesticity.

Mythili, her spirit strengthened by her unwavering pursuit of her dreams, refused. *"Love that demands you sacrifice yourself is not love at all."*

She explained her passion for music, her dreams of a career as a vocalist, her unwavering commitment to her artistic calling. The groom, unable to comprehend her aspirations or accept her defiance of tradition, withdrew his proposal, leaving Mythili's family devastated and their reputation in the village seemingly tarnished.

The Support of the Soul

Amidst the storm of disapproval and disappointment, Mythili found solace in the quiet support of her grandmother, a woman whose wisdom was as deep as the village well and whose love for her granddaughter transcended the boundaries of tradition and societal expectations.

"The river of life flows in many directions," her grandmother counseled, her voice gentle but firm. "Let each choose their own course."

She reminded Mythili of her inner strength, her unwavering passion, and the importance of staying true to herself, regardless of the obstacles she might face. *"The support of one soul can outweigh the disapproval of many."*

The Blossom of Happiness

Mythili, her spirit renewed by her grandmother's unwavering belief in her, continued her pursuit of her musical dreams. She finally gained admission to the prestigious music school in Chennai, her talent recognized, her dedication rewarded. Years of perseverance and unwavering commitment culminated in her first solo performance, a moment of triumph that marked the beginning of her artistic journey.

Her voice, filled with emotion and the wisdom gained through her struggles, captivated the audience, her melodies resonating with the depths of their souls. She wasn't just singing; she was telling her story, the story of a young woman who dared to defy expectations, who chose the path of her heart, and who found happiness in pursuing her passion. *"Happiness is not found in the approval of others, but in the acceptance of oneself."*

The Jasmine's Unfolding

Mythili went on to become a renowned Carnatic vocalist, her music touching the hearts of thousands, her voice a testament to the power of self-belief and the unwavering pursuit of one's dreams. She had chosen her own path, faced criticism, overcome setbacks, and ultimately found fulfillment in staying true to herself.

Her journey was like the unfolding of a jasmine flower, its fragrance spreading slowly but surely, its beauty captivating all who encountered it. It was a reminder that true happiness lies not in conforming to societal expectations, but in embracing one's unique destiny and allowing one's spirit to blossom in its own time and in its own way. *"Like the jasmine that unfolds its fragrance in its own time, your true self will blossom when you embrace your own unique destiny."*

Moral of the Story:

"Life is not about pleasing everyone; it's about having the courage to be yourself, to pursue your passions, and to create your own path. Choose what makes you happy, for in the end, your happiness is your responsibility. Those who truly love you will understand and support your choices; those who don't, don't matter."

XXVI
The Lost Reflection

"The greatest loss is not of love, but of the self in the pursuit of love."

A Journey Back to the Self

The Quiet Sacrifice

In the bustling city of Hyderabad, where ambition and tradition intertwined, Anika's love for Aarav blossomed like a delicate jasmine flower, its fragrance filling her world with a sweetness that masked the subtle sacrifices she made along the way. From the moment their hearts intertwined, she found herself rearranging her life, her priorities, her very identity to accommodate his needs, his desires, his vision for their future.

At first, it seemed natural, an unspoken dance of compromise and accommodation that she believed was the essence of true love. She would cancel plans with her friends if he needed her, adjust her schedule to align with his, and slowly, almost imperceptibly, let go of the small things that had once brought her joy and fulfillment.

It wasn't a dramatic transformation, a sudden shift in her personality or her aspirations. It was a gradual erosion, a quiet fading of her own desires, her own dreams, her own sense of self. She stopped painting, the vibrant canvases that had once adorned her walls now gathering dust in a forgotten corner, because their weekend trips were always planned around Aarav's interests, his love for adventure and exploration overshadowing her own artistic pursuits.

She no longer listened to her favorite music, the melodies that had once stirred her soul now replaced by the silence he preferred in the car, his need for quiet contemplation taking precedence over her desire for vibrant expression. And she adjusted her dreams, her aspirations for a career as a writer now relegated to the back burner, her focus shifting to supporting Aarav's ambitions, her own goals fading into the background like a forgotten melody. *"Love is not meant to shrink you. Love, when true, expands you."*

The Fading Self

Months turned into years, the seasons changing, the city growing around them, and Anika barely noticed how much of herself had been lost in the process of loving Aarav. She believed she was happy, her happiness defined by his success, his contentment, his approval. But deep down, a nagging emptiness gnawed at her soul, a quiet whisper of discontent that she tried to ignore, to bury beneath the layers of responsibility and self-sacrifice.

Then, one evening, as she was tidying up their bookshelf, a small, dust-covered canvas tumbled from its hiding place behind a stack of forgotten novels. It was one of her old paintings, a vibrant explosion of colors and textures, a testament to the passion and creativity that had once flowed through her veins.

She stared at the painting, her heart aching with a longing for the woman she had once been, the artist whose spirit had been dimmed by the shadows of compromise and self-neglect.

"When was the last time I painted?" she whispered to herself, the question echoing through the silent room, its answer a painful reminder of the sacrifices she had made in the name of love.

She looked around their meticulously decorated home, noticing for the first time that nothing in it truly reflected her own tastes, her own personality, her own unique essence. It was all Aarav's world – his books, his choices, his preferences. And she, in her eagerness to please and her fear of disrupting their seemingly perfect life, had willingly, unconsciously molded herself to fit into his world, her own identity fading into the background like a forgotten melody.

The Awakening

That night, as she lay beside Aarav, his rhythmic breathing a comforting counterpoint to the racing thoughts that filled her mind, a question pierced through the silence, its clarity startling her awake. "Who am I outside of this relationship?"

It was a terrifying question, one she had never dared to ask herself before. The answer, she realized with a growing sense of dread, was that she didn't know. The Anika who had once possessed dreams, passions, and a life of her own had faded into someone who merely existed in relation to someone else, her identity defined by her role as a wife, a supporter, a shadow of her former self.

The next morning, driven by a newfound determination to reclaim her lost identity, Anika did something she hadn't done in years – she picked up her paintbrush. At first, the strokes were hesitant, uncertain, as if she were trying to remember a language she had long forgotten. But with each stroke, with each splash of color on the canvas, she felt a small part of herself returning, her spirit reawakening, her soul finding its voice once more.

When Aarav walked in, his brow furrowed in surprise, his words a testament to how far she had allowed herself to fade. "I didn't know you still painted," he remarked casually, his tone revealing his obliviousness to the sacrifices she had made.

Anika's heart ached at his words, their casualness a stark reminder of how completely she had erased herself from their shared narrative. "I used to," she replied quietly, her voice trembling slightly but her resolve firming with each word. "And I think it's time I start again."

The Rebirth

Reclaiming herself was not an easy journey. It required setting boundaries, saying "no" when she had once habitually said "yes," and rediscovering the activities, the passions, the simple joys that had once made her soul sing. She began to read again, the words of her favorite authors filling her mind with new ideas and perspectives. She started exploring the city on her own, her footsteps leading her to hidden corners and forgotten treasures. And she painted, her canvases now a reflection of her own inner world, her own unique vision, her own vibrant spirit.

As Anika grew, as she reclaimed her space and her identity, something shifted in her relationship with Aarav. He noticed the change in her, the quiet confidence that now radiated from her being, the spark that had returned to her eyes. At first, he resisted, his ego bruised by her newfound independence, his sense of control threatened by her refusal to conform to his expectations. But love, real love, the kind that endures, is not about possession or control; it's about two complete individuals choosing to walk together, their paths intertwined yet their individuality respected and celebrated.

One evening, as Anika stood before a completed painting, her first in years, a masterpiece that reflected her journey of self-discovery and her reawakened spirit, Aarav came and stood beside her, his gaze drawn to the vibrant colors and evocative forms that danced across the canvas. "It's beautiful," he said, his voice filled with genuine admiration.

Anika turned to him, her eyes sparkling with a newfound joy, her smile a testament to the transformative power of self-love and self-acceptance. For the first time in a long time, she felt whole, not because of him, but because she had finally found herself again.

The Lesson

The most painful loss is not the loss of someone we love, but the loss of ourselves in the process of loving them. Love should never require us to dim our light, to silence our voice, or to sacrifice our dreams. True love, the kind that nourishes and sustains, allows us to be fully, unapologetically ourselves, our individuality celebrated, our spirits soaring.

So, if you ever find yourself shrinking, fading, disappearing for the sake of love, stop. Take a step back, breathe deeply, and reclaim yourself. Remember the person you were before the world told you who you should be. Embrace your passions, pursue your dreams, and never apologize for being fully, authentically you. Because the love you so freely give to others, you deserve that too.

Moral of the Story:

"You are not meant to fade into the background of someone else's story. You are meant to take up space, to be seen, to be heard, to be loved for who you truly are – not just for what you can give."

XXVII

The Courage to Bloom

*"The greatest journey is the one we take to discover
the uncharted territories within ourselves."*

The Whispers of Tradition In the heart of a small village nestled amidst the rolling hills of Tamil Nadu, where the scent of jasmine blossoms filled the air and the ancient banyan tree stood as a silent witness to the passage of time, Maya's spirit yearned for a horizon beyond the familiar boundaries of her world. She was a young woman of intelligence and ambition, her heart filled with dreams that whispered of a different path, a path that diverged from the well-trodden road laid out for her by tradition and societal expectations.

From the time she was a young girl, the whispers of her elders had painted a clear picture of her future. Marriage, children, and a life dedicated to the hearth and home – these were the pillars upon which a woman's life was built, the foundations of a fulfilling and respectable existence. But Maya, her soul stirred by a restless curiosity and an unquenchable thirst for knowledge, envisioned a different destiny, one where her spirit could soar beyond the confines of her village and her potential could blossom into its fullest expression.

The Courage to Bloom

Maya's yearning for a life beyond the traditional roles assigned to women was a discordant note in the symphony of her community, a whisper of rebellion against the comfortable and familiar. She loved her family, her village, the traditions that had shaped her identity. But she also knew that her heart's melody could not be silenced, that her spirit could not be confined to the narrow path laid out for her. *"The truest path is the one you carve for yourself."*

One sweltering afternoon, as the sun beat down on the parched earth and the villagers sought refuge in the cool shade of the banyan tree, Maya sat lost in thought, her brow furrowed with the weight of her unspoken desires. Nana Rao, the village storyteller, a man whose wisdom was as deep as the roots of the banyan tree and whose eyes twinkled with the knowledge of a thousand tales, approached her, his presence a comforting balm in the midst of her inner turmoil.

He sat beside her, offering a companionable silence before speaking, his voice raspy but gentle, like the rustling of leaves in the evening breeze.

"Maya," he began, "I see the storm brewing in your heart. The path laid out for you is well-trodden, safe, and familiar. But your heart, like a restless bird, yearns for a different sky."

Maya looked at him, her eyes filled with tears of gratitude and relief. "Nana Rao," she confessed, her voice trembling with emotion, "I feel torn. I love my family, my village, the life I have always known. But this... this longing inside me, it won't let me rest. It whispers of a different path, a path that leads beyond the boundaries of our traditions."

Nana Rao smiled, his wrinkles deepening with the warmth of understanding. "My child," he said, "the greatest courage lies in choosing yourself, over and over again. The river of life flows forward, not backward. Growth is not always comfortable, but it is necessary. It is how we shed the old skin of conformity and discover the true essence of who we are meant to be."

The Stone and the Tree

He picked up a small, smooth stone from the ground and handed it to Maya.

"Hold this," he instructed. "Feel its weight, its texture. *This stone, like your life, is shaped by the forces that act upon it. Sometimes, those forces are gentle, like the caress of the wind. Sometimes, they are harsh, like the raging river. But it is through these forces, through the challenges and the triumphs, that the stone becomes smooth, becomes beautiful, becomes its truest self."*

Maya, her fingers tracing the contours of the stone, felt its weight grounding her, its smoothness a reminder of the resilience that lay within her.

"But what if I fail?" she whispered, her voice laced with fear.

Nana Rao chuckled, his eyes twinkling with amusement. *"Failure, my dear, is but a stepping stone on the path to success. It is in our stumbles that we learn to walk, in our falls that we learn to rise. The important thing is to never stop moving forward, to never stop believing in the possibilities that lie ahead."*

He pointed to the majestic banyan tree that towered above them, its branches reaching towards the sky, its roots anchoring it firmly to the earth.

"Look at this magnificent tree, Maya," he said. *"Its roots are strong, connecting it to the wisdom of its ancestors, the traditions of its land. But its branches reach towards the sky, always seeking the light, always striving for growth and expansion. Be like this tree, Maya. Honor your roots, but never be afraid to reach for the stars."*

The Courage to Choose

Maya held the stone tightly in her hand, Nana Rao's words echoing through her heart, their wisdom illuminating her path. She realized that loving her family and her village did not necessitate the sacrifice of her own dreams. She could honor her heritage while still pursuing her own unique destiny, her own path towards self-discovery and fulfillment.

From that day forward, Maya began to choose herself, over and over again. She spoke to her family about her desire to learn, to explore the world beyond their village, to discover the hidden melodies within her own soul. It was a difficult conversation, filled with tears, doubts, and the weight of generations of tradition. But her parents, witnessing her unwavering determination and the depth of her passion, eventually came to understand and support her dreams.

She left the village, not in rebellion or defiance, but with their blessings and the knowledge that she carried their love and support with her, no matter where her journey might lead.

The Journey of Self-Discovery

Maya's path was not without its challenges. She faced setbacks, moments of doubt, and the loneliness of navigating an unfamiliar world. But she remembered Nana Rao's words, the weight of the stone in her hand, and the image of the banyan tree reaching for the sky. She persevered, her spirit strengthened by each obstacle she overcame, her resolve fueled by her unwavering belief in her own potential.

She learned, she grew, and she eventually returned to her village, not as the girl who had left, but as a woman who had embraced her own unique journey, who had discovered the strength and resilience that lay within her.

The Teacher and the Tree

Maya became a teacher, sharing her knowledge and experiences with the young people of her village, inspiring them to dream big, to challenge limitations, and to pursue their own paths with courage and determination. And under the shade of the old banyan tree, where her own journey had begun, she would gather the children and remind them of the wisdom she had gleaned along the way.

"You are worthy of everything you've ever wanted," she would tell them, her voice filled with conviction. *"Have the courage to choose yourself, over and over again. Honor your roots, but never be afraid to reach for the stars."*

Moral of the Story:

"The greatest journey is the one we take to discover the uncharted territories within ourselves.
Have the courage to choose yourself, to pursue your dreams, and to defy the expectations that seek to confine you.
Embrace your potential, for it is in the blossoming of your own unique spirit that you will find true happiness and fulfillment."

XXVIII
The Inherited Ideology

"The most enduring inheritance is not wealth or possessions, but the values and ideals that shape our souls."

The Weight of Legacy

In the quiet confines of his study, Rohan, a political titan whose influence stretched across the vast landscape of Uttar Pradesh, found himself drawn to the familiar comfort of his father's old library. The scent of aged paper and leather-bound books filled the air, a nostalgic aroma that transported him back to his childhood, to a time when the world was simpler, the boundaries of possibility less defined.

He ran a calloused finger along the worn spine of "Das Kapital," its pages brittle with age, its text a testament to the enduring power of ideas. It was a book that had shaped his father's worldview, a book that had sparked countless debates under the shade of the village banyan tree, its words echoing through the corridors of Rohan's memory.

His father, Anand, a fervent communist and a dedicated schoolteacher, had seen in Marx not just a historical figure, but a prophet of social justice, a visionary whose ideas held the key to a more equitable and just society. He had instilled in Rohan a deep respect for the collective, a belief in the power of unity to overcome oppression, and a commitment to fighting for the rights of the marginalized and the voiceless.

"Remember, Rohan," Anand had often said, his eyes burning with conviction, *"the world is not built on individual glory, but on collective strength. From each according to his ability, to each according to his need."*

Rohan, now a seasoned politician, a master of the art of compromise and negotiation, stood in stark contrast to his father's humble life and unwavering idealism. He had built an empire of influence, his network of connections stretching across the state, his name whispered in the corridors of power. He was a "tycoon," as the newspapers called him, a pragmatist who understood the currency of power and the delicate dance of political maneuvering.

Echoes of Wisdom

Yet, despite his own success and his embrace of a more pragmatic approach to politics, Rohan could not escape the echoes of his father's teachings. The words that had once seemed idealistic and impractical now resonated with a newfound clarity, their wisdom seeping into the core of his being.

"Don't waste your time worrying about things you can't change," Anand had often counseled, his voice a calming presence in the midst of youthful frustration.

Rohan, reflecting on his father's words, understood their deeper meaning. It wasn't about apathy or resignation; it was about focusing one's energy and efforts on the things one could influence, on making a tangible difference in the world, however small it might seem.

He remembered the countless nights his father had spent organizing village cooperatives, rallying the farmers and laborers against the exploitative practices of the landlords, his efforts often met with setbacks and disappointments. But Anand had never given up, his spirit fueled by an unwavering belief in the power of collective action to create a more just and equitable society.

"Work hard, but don't forget to live," Anand had also taught him, his words a reminder that life was not just about struggle and sacrifice, but also about finding joy in the simple things, in the shared moments of laughter, connection, and community.

Rohan, in his relentless pursuit of power and influence, had often forgotten this simple truth. He had allowed his ambition to consume him, neglecting the human element, the simple pleasures that made life worth living. He had sacrificed his personal relationships, his health, and his own well-being on the altar of political success.

The Unwavering Support

"No matter what happens, I've got your back," Anand had always assured him, his words a bedrock of support, a promise of unwavering loyalty and unconditional love.

Anand believed in solidarity, in standing with the marginalized, in fighting for those who had no voice. Rohan, in his political ascent, had often compromised, making alliances with those he once despised, justifying his actions as necessary pragmatism in the pursuit of the greater good.

But as he reflected on his father's words, he realized that true strength lay not in compromising one's values, but in upholding them, even in the face of adversity, even when it meant sacrificing personal gain for the sake of those he had pledged to serve.

The Transformation

One evening, addressing a massive rally, Rohan found himself deviating from his carefully prepared speech. The words that flowed from his lips were not the usual platitudes and promises, but a passionate plea for social justice, a call for a return to the values that had shaped his father's life and his own childhood.

"We speak of progress," he declared, his voice resonating through the crowd, *"but what is progress if it leaves half our people behind? The philosophers have only interpreted the world, in various ways; the point is to change it."*

He quoted Marx, his father's words mingling with the revolutionary spirit of the past, their combined power electrifying the audience. He spoke of a new kind of politics, one that combined the pragmatism of the present with the idealism of the past, a politics that sought to create a more just and equitable society for all.

"We must build a system where opportunity is not a privilege, but a right," he proclaimed, his voice echoing through the vast gathering. *"Where the strength of the nation is measured not by the wealth of a few, but by the well-being of all."*

The crowd, accustomed to his usual rhetoric, was taken aback by his passionate appeal for social justice, his words a stark contrast to the self-serving pronouncements of most politicians. But within their surprise, a spark of hope ignited, a recognition that perhaps this leader, this man of power and influence, was different, that he carried within him the seeds of his father's idealism, a yearning for a better world.

The Legacy

Later that evening, in the quiet solitude of his study, Rohan gazed at a faded photograph of his father, his eyes filled with a mixture of gratitude and determination.

"Dad," he whispered, his voice thick with emotion, "I still hear you everywhere."

He realized that his political journey was not a betrayal of his father's legacy, but a complex and evolving dialogue with it. He was a product of his time, a political tycoon who understood the realities of power and compromise. But he also carried within him the seeds of his father's idealism, a yearning for a more just and equitable society, a world where everyone had the opportunity to thrive.

He knew the road ahead would be fraught with challenges, with compromises and contradictions. But he also knew that, in some way, his father's spirit was guiding him, reminding him that true power lay not in personal glory, but in the pursuit of a better future for all.

Moral of the story:

"The most enduring inheritance is not wealth or possessions, but the values and ideals that shape our souls. The legacy of those who came before us lives on in the choices we make, the actions we take, and the dreams we pursue. Embrace the wisdom of your ancestors, honor their sacrifices, and use your own unique talents and opportunities to create a better world for generations to come."

XXIX
The Halls of Silence

"The river of justice must flow, even if it means carving a new path through the mountains of opposition."

The River and the Ocean of Justice

In the bustling city of Hyderabad, where the pursuit of justice often clashed with the harsh realities of power and corruption, Arjun, a young and idealistic advocate, embarked on his legal career with a heart filled with hope and a burning desire to make a difference. He had chosen law not for the allure of fame or fortune, but to be a voice for the voiceless, to champion the cause of those who had been wronged, to bring justice to those who had been denied it.

His journey had begun with a dream, a vision of a world where the scales of justice were balanced, where the law served as a shield for the innocent and a sword against the wicked. But as he stepped into the hallowed halls of the district court, he was confronted with a stark reality, a world where the pursuit of justice was often overshadowed by the pursuit of power, wealth, and personal gain.

Arjun's mentor, Senior Advocate Sharma, a man hardened by years of legal battles and disillusioned by the compromises and betrayals he had witnessed, offered no guidance, no encouragement, no support. The other advocates, their suits impeccably tailored, their connections well-established, scoffed at Arjun's idealism, their laughter echoing through the corridors of the court like a cruel mockery of his dreams.

"Justice for the poor?" they sneered. "You'll starve before you see that."

Arjun's own pockets were as empty as his client list. He couldn't afford to waive his fees, couldn't even afford a decent meal most days. The river of his idealism, once a raging torrent, began to stagnate, its currents slowed by the weight of disillusionment and despair. He looked back at his journey, the years of study, the sacrifices he had made, the burning desire to make a difference, and then forward at the vast, unforgiving ocean of the legal system, its depths teeming with sharks and its currents treacherous and unpredictable.

The Clerk's Wisdom

One evening, as the sun dipped below the horizon, painting the sky in hues of orange and purple, Arjun sat on the steps of the district court, his head in his hands, his spirit weary. Mr. Rao, a veteran court clerk who had witnessed countless legal battles and the rise and fall of many advocates, approached him, his weathered face etched with the wisdom of experience and a quiet empathy for the young man's struggles.

"You seem troubled, young man," Mr. Rao remarked, his voice gentle and concerned.

Arjun, his heart heavy with frustration and despair, poured out his soul to the old clerk, his words tumbling over each other in a torrent of disillusionment. He spoke of his dreams of justice, the harsh realities of the legal system, the cynicism of his colleagues, and the crushing weight of his own financial struggles.

Mr. Rao listened patiently, his eyes filled with understanding and a flicker of recognition. He had seen countless young advocates like Arjun, their idealism battered by the harsh winds of reality, their spirits dimmed by the shadows of compromise and corruption.

"I understand your struggles, Arjun," Mr. Rao said, his voice filled with compassion. "But you must not give up on your ideals. Remember the words of Nani Palkhivala, the great jurist who fought tirelessly for the rights of the common man, who said, *'The law is not an end in itself, but a means to an end, and that end is the welfare of the people.' You have the power to make a difference,*

Arjun, even if it seems like a small difference in the grand scheme of things."

He continued, his voice gaining strength, "Remember the legacy of Justice Krishna Iyer, who championed the cause of social justice and used the law as a tool to uplift the oppressed. He once said, *'The law is not an abstraction, but a living force that must be used to protect the weak and the vulnerable.'* You can be that force, Arjun. You can *be the voice of those who have been silenced, the champion of those who have been denied justice."*

Arjun, his spirit rekindled by Mr. Rao's words, felt a surge of hope coursing through him. He realized that he wasn't alone in his struggle, that there were others who had walked this path before him, who had faced similar challenges, and who had emerged victorious.

"Think of the countless lawyers and judges who have fought for justice throughout history," Mr. Rao continued, his voice filled with passion. "Think of Mahatma Gandhi, who used the law as a tool to fight for India's independence. Think of Nelson Mandela, who spent decades in prison for his beliefs but never gave up on his dream of a just and equitable society. Think of Ruth Bader Ginsburg, who fought tirelessly for gender equality and inspired generations of women to pursue their dreams."

The Turning Tide

Arjun, inspired by the stories of these legal giants, felt a renewed sense of purpose. He realized that the pursuit of justice was not a solitary endeavor, but a collective struggle that spanned generations and continents. He was part of a long and noble tradition, a tradition of fighting for what is right, even when the odds seem insurmountable.

He began to focus his energy on cases where he could make a real difference, where he could expose the cracks in the system and bring justice to those who had been denied it. He meticulously prepared his arguments, his sharp intellect dissecting the complexities of the law, his passion for justice fueling his every word. He quoted from the Constitution, from the writings of India's founding fathers, reminding the court of the principles of equality, fairness, and the fundamental rights of every citizen.

Slowly but surely, the tide began to turn. People started noticing Arjun's dedication, his unwavering commitment to justice, his refusal to compromise his integrity. He won a few landmark cases, exposing corruption, challenging the status quo, and bringing hope to those who had been denied it. The laughter of his colleagues, once a source of discouragement, now turned into grudging respect, their cynicism challenged by his unwavering idealism.

The Ocean of Justice

Arjun realized that he wasn't just a young advocate struggling against a system; he was becoming a part of something larger, a force for change within the vast ocean of justice. He understood that the journey was not about reaching a destination, but about becoming the change he wished to see in the world.

He knew his path was long and arduous, but he walked it with the conviction that he was not just a river flowing towards the sea, but a wave within the ocean itself, his every action contributing to the ebb and flow of justice, his every victory a ripple that would spread outward, creating a more equitable and just world for all.

Moral of the story:

"The pursuit of justice is a journey, not a destination. It is a constant struggle against the forces of corruption, inequality, and oppression. But even in the face of adversity, we must never give up on our ideals, for it is through our unwavering commitment to justice that we create a better world for ourselves and for generations to come."

XXX
The Forgotten Manuscript

"The true measure of a leader lies not in their victories, but in the indomitable spirit they ignite within their people."

A Tale of Subhas Chandra Bose's Vision

The Whispers of Destiny

In the heart of Rangoon, the year was 1944. The monsoon season had just ended, leaving behind a city draped in emerald green and the lingering scent of rain-soaked earth. Subhas Chandra Bose, the charismatic leader known as Netaji, sat alone in his dimly lit office, the weight of a nation's hopes and dreams resting heavily on his shoulders.

The Indian National Army (INA), his brainchild, his passion, his unwavering commitment to freeing India from the clutches of the British Empire, was poised on the precipice of a decisive battle. The Burma campaign, a daring gamble to liberate India's eastern territories and pave the way for a final assault on the heart of the Raj, hung in the balance.

Netaji, his brow furrowed in concentration, traced the lines on the worn map spread across his desk, his fingers lingering over the strategic points, his mind envisioning the movements of troops, the clash of arms, the sacrifices that lay ahead. The air crackled with anticipation, the silence punctuated by the distant sounds of marching boots and the faint strains of patriotic songs echoing through the humid night.

A flicker of movement in the corner of his eye caught his attention. A tattered manuscript, its leather binding cracked and worn, lay half-hidden beneath a stack of official documents, its presence a whisper from a forgotten past. Intrigued, Netaji reached for it, his fingers gently brushing away the layers of dust that had accumulated over time. The manuscript, its pages brittle with age, its ink faded but still legible, seemed to beckon him, its secrets whispering promises of a destiny yet to be fulfilled.

"Rahul," Netaji called out, his voice cutting through the stillness of the room.

Rahul, his trusted aide and confidante, a brilliant young linguist who had dedicated his life to the cause of India's freedom, hurried into the office, his eyes filled with concern. "Yes, Netaji?"

"Can you decipher this?" Netaji asked, handing him the mysterious manuscript.

Rahul carefully examined the text, his brow furrowed in concentration as he traced the unfamiliar characters with his fingertips. A flicker of recognition crossed his face, his eyes widening with excitement.

"Netaji," he exclaimed, his voice hushed with awe, "this is written in an ancient script from Bengal, a script that has been lost to the ages. It speaks of a prophecy, a leader who will arise to unite the fragmented lands of Bharat, to break the chains of foreign rule, and to lead our people to freedom. It seems... it speaks of you."

Netaji's heart pounded in his chest, a mixture of anticipation and trepidation coursing through his veins. He had always believed that his mission was divinely ordained, that he was destined to play a pivotal role in India's struggle for independence. But this discovery, this ancient prophecy that seemed to foretell his own rise to leadership, filled him with a profound sense of responsibility, a realization that his actions would not only shape the present, but also echo through the corridors of history.

"I am no prophet, Rahul," he said, his voice steady despite the emotions swirling within him. "I am but a servant of the people, a humble instrument in the hands of destiny. My duty is clear, my path illuminated by the sacrifices of countless freedom fighters who have come before me. *Freedom is not a gift to be bestowed; it is a right to be earned, a destiny to be forged through courage, sacrifice, and unwavering determination."*

Rahul, inspired by his leader's humility and unwavering commitment to the cause, nodded in agreement. He understood that Netaji's strength lay not in his belief in prophecy, but in his unwavering faith in the power of the human spirit to overcome adversity and achieve the impossible.

The Manuscript's Wisdom

In the days that followed, amidst the relentless demands of war and the constant threat of danger, Netaji found solace in the ancient manuscript. He would pore over its pages late into the night, the flickering lamplight casting dancing shadows on the walls, his mind absorbed in the tales of courage, resilience, and sacrifice that unfolded before him.

Rahul, his linguistic skills proving invaluable, translated the text, revealing a treasure trove of wisdom and inspiration from India's forgotten past. The stories spoke of legendary warriors who had fought for their freedom against insurmountable odds, of visionary leaders who had united their people against oppression, and of ordinary men and women who had sacrificed everything for the dream of a free and independent India.

One particular passage resonated deeply with Netaji, its words etching themselves into his memory: *"The leader who walks through fire will forge an unbreakable spirit among his people. His voice will echo through the ages, even when his form fades from the earth."*

Netaji closed his eyes, the words of the prophecy swirling through his mind, their meaning resonating with his own experiences and aspirations. He thought of his INA soldiers, their unwavering loyalty, their willingness to lay down their lives for the cause of freedom. He thought of the countless nameless martyrs who had paved the path he now walked, their sacrifices a testament to the enduring spirit of India's struggle for independence.

He turned to Rahul, his eyes filled with a newfound determination. "This manuscript is not just a relic, Rahul," he declared, his voice echoing through the quiet room. "It is a testament to our people's indomitable spirit, a reminder of the sacrifices that have been made and the battles that have been fought. It must be preserved, not for me, but for future generations, so that they may draw strength from the legacy of our ancestors and continue the fight for a free and independent India."

Rahul, his heart filled with admiration for his leader's vision, nodded in agreement. But a flicker of concern crossed his face. "Netaji," he hesitated, "what if the British discover it? They will destroy it, as they have destroyed so much of our heritage, our history, our identity."

Netaji's eyes burned with an unwavering resolve. "Then we shall guard it with our lives, Rahul," he vowed. *"A nation's soul cannot be extinguished as long as its people remember their legacy, their history, their identity.* We will protect this manuscript, not just for ourselves, but for the generations to come, for the India that will one day be free."

The Call to Action

The manuscript became a source of inspiration for Netaji, its words fueling his determination, its stories reminding him of the sacrifices that had been made and the battles that lay ahead. In his speeches to the INA soldiers, he wove the manuscript's lessons into his fiery rhetoric, his words igniting a spark of hope and defiance in the hearts of his followers.

"Give me blood, and I will give you freedom!" he thundered during one rally, his voice echoing across the vast parade ground, his words electrifying the assembled troops. *"It is blood alone that can pay the price of freedom. But it is a price we must be willing to pay, for the freedom of our nation is worth more than any individual life."*

The soldiers, young and old, men and women from all walks of life, united by their shared dream of a free India, roared their approval, their spirits lifted by Netaji's unwavering conviction and the power of his words.

But Netaji, ever the pragmatist, knew that the road to freedom was paved with obstacles and fraught with danger. The INA faced immense challenges, their resources limited, their enemies powerful and relentless. Whispers of betrayal and disunity among some of their allies had begun to surface, casting a shadow of doubt over their mission.

Yet, Netaji remained unshaken, his resolve strengthened by the wisdom of the ancients and the unwavering support of his followers. One evening, while addressing a secret council of INA leaders, he shared the prophecy from the forgotten manuscript, its words a testament to the collective spirit of their struggle.

"This is not about one man's journey," he emphasized, his voice filled with conviction. *"This is about a nation awakening from centuries of slumber. Each*

of you is a part of this prophecy, for the spirit of Bharat resides in every heart that beats for freedom."

The Unseen Hand of Destiny

As the tides of war turned against them, and the threat of capture loomed large, Netaji made a decision that would define his legacy and ensure the survival of the manuscript that had become a symbol of India's indomitable spirit.

"Rahul," he instructed, his voice firm but filled with emotion, "take this manuscript to a place where no conqueror can reach. Hide it, bury it, protect it with your life, but ensure that it is never lost, that its wisdom and its spirit live on to inspire future generations."

Rahul hesitated, his loyalty to Netaji battling with his concern for the safety of the manuscript. "But Netaji," he protested, "what about you? This manuscript feels like your story, your legacy."

Netaji placed a reassuring hand on Rahul's shoulder, his eyes filled with a profound understanding of the sacrifices that leadership demanded. *"A leader is nothing without his people, Rahul,"* he said. *"My story is the story of every Indian who dreams of freedom, who fights for justice, who refuses to bow down to oppression.* Go now, my friend. *The time for words is over; the time for action has come.* Protect this manuscript, and you protect the soul of our nation."

The Legacy

Rahul, his heart heavy but his resolve strengthened by Netaji's unwavering faith in him, carried out his leader's orders. He disappeared into the shadows, the manuscript safely hidden away, its fate unknown, its secrets preserved for a future generation to discover and draw inspiration from.

Years later, as the British Raj finally crumbled under the weight of India's struggle for independence, the echoes of Netaji's words continued to inspire and motivate those who fought for a better world.

"Give me blood, and I will give you freedom," he had declared, his voice a clarion call that resonated through the ages, a reminder that the price of liberty is often paid in blood, sweat, and tears.

Though Subhas Chandra Bose's ultimate fate remains shrouded in mystery, his legacy lives on, his spirit enshrined in the hearts of millions who continue to strive for a just and equitable society. The forgotten manuscript, a testament to India's indomitable spirit and its unwavering pursuit of freedom, serves as a reminder that the fight for justice is eternal, and that the greatest leaders are those who awaken the spirit of resistance within their people.

As India celebrates only the birth anniversary of this extraordinary leader, let us remember not just his actions, but his vision, a vision that transcended time and space, igniting a revolution of the soul that continues to inspire and guide us today.

"The future belongs to those who can dare to dream of a free tomorrow. Let us honor Netaji not with words, but with deeds that carry forward his unyielding spirit of sacrifice and courage."

Moral of the story:

"The true legacy of a leader lies not in their personal achievements, but in the spirit they ignite within their people, the dreams they inspire, and the sacrifices they make for the greater good. Even in the face of overwhelming odds, the fight for justice and freedom must continue, for it is through our collective struggle that we forge a better future for ourselves and for generations to come."

Afterword

As I bring this collection of stories to a close, I am filled with a sense of gratitude and accomplishment. "The YS Tales: Whispers of Wisdom" has been a labor of love, a journey of exploration into the depths of human experience and the enduring power of wisdom.

These stories have allowed me to connect with my own heritage, to delve into the rich tapestry of Indian culture and spirituality, and to share the lessons I have learned along the way. They have challenged me to confront my own beliefs, to question my assumptions, and to embrace the complexities and contradictions that make us human.

I hope that these stories have resonated with you, dear reader, that they have sparked your imagination, touched your heart, and left you with a deeper understanding of yourself and the world around you. I hope that they have inspired you to seek wisdom in unexpected places, to embrace your own unique journey, and to never give up on the pursuit of your dreams.

The journey of writing "The YS Tales" has been a transformative one for me, and I am grateful for the opportunity to share these stories with you. I believe that stories have the power to heal, to inspire, and to connect us to something larger than ourselves. They remind us that we are not alone in our struggles, that our experiences are shared, and that there is always hope, even in the darkest of times.

As you close this book, I invite you to carry the whispers of wisdom with you, to let them guide you on your own path, and to share them with others. May these stories continue to spark conversations, to inspire action, and to contribute to the creation of a more just, compassionate, and enlightened world.

ACKNOWLEDGEMENT

The journey of writing "The YS Tales: Whispers of Wisdom" has been a long and winding one, and I am grateful for the many people who have supported me along the way.

First and foremost, I would like to thank my family and friends for their unwavering love, encouragement, and patience. Your belief in me and my work has been a constant source of inspiration.

I am also deeply indebted to my mentors and colleagues in the legal profession, whose wisdom and guidance have shaped my understanding of justice, ethics, and the power of the law to create a better world.

I would like to express my gratitude to the countless authors, philosophers, and spiritual leaders whose works have inspired me and whose words have found their way into the pages of this book.

Finally, I would like to thank you, dear reader, for taking the time to explore these stories and for allowing me to share my vision with you. Your willingness to engage with these tales and to embrace their wisdom is the greatest reward I could ask for.

May the whispers of wisdom continue to guide us all on our journeys.

ABOUT THE AUTHOR

Y.S. Yadav

Y.S.Yadav is a distinguished advocate, author, and social activist with an unwavering commitment to legal empowerment, social justice, and the preservation of cultural heritage. He practices law at the High Court of Andhra Pradesh and serves as the National President of Service Civil International (SCI-India), National Secretary of the Central Human Rights Organisation, National Executive Member of All India Yadav Mahasabha, and State Secretary of the Indian Association of Lawyers (IAL), Andhra Pradesh.

His passion for writing is evident in his diverse body of work, which spans the realms of law, history, and social reform. He has a unique ability to blend legal insights with compelling storytelling, making complex issues accessible and engaging for a wide range of readers. His published books include "The Constitution Speaks: Stories of India's Top 25 Landmark Judgments," "Golla Mandapam," "Gopika Geetham," and "When Gods Walked the Sacred Hills: LEGENDS OF SESHACHALAM." His recent publication, "THE ASH-BORN WARRIORS: The Naga Sadhus and the Secrets of the Maha Kumbh," delves into the fascinating world of the Naga Sadhus and their role in Indian culture and spirituality. His upcoming works, "My Fate - A Journey Beyond Boundaries and Beliefs" and "The Gambit of Gandhara," promise to be thought-provoking additions to his literary repertoire.

Beyond his legal and literary pursuits, Y.S.Yadav is a passionate advocate for the rights of marginalized communities, particularly the OBCs. He champions policy reforms, cultural heritage preservation, and social justice initiatives, striving to create a more equitable and inclusive society.

A firm believer in the mantra "Rise for Rights and Stand for Justice," his mission is to educate, empower, and inspire readers to engage with the law, history, and social issues that shape our world.